Sinful Desires

Thanks,
Enjoy

A NOVEL BY

Ty Goode

Ty Goode

This is a work of fiction. Any names, places, characters or events are purely a product of the author's imagination or are used fictitiously, and any resemblance to actual persons living or dead is entirely coincidental.

Copyright © 2004 By Ty Goode
Library of Congress Control Number: 2004099845
ISBN: 0-9758602-0-8

Text formation by Jonathan Gullery
Cover graphics by Nannette Buchanan
Cover concept by Ty Goode

Request for permission to make copies or any part of the work should be mailed to

Tytam Publishing
   c/oTy Goode
PO Box 1903
Newark, N J 07101
E-mail: TyGoode1@aol.com
Website: www.TyGoode.com

Printed in the USA.

Dedication

This book is dedicated to the memory
of my father, Mr. John Lee Stokes.
Meet you on the other side daddy

Acknowledgements

First and foremost I'd like to thank my higher power, Jesus Christ, with whom all things are possible.

I'm so glad that I don't have the kind of friends and relatives that need to see their name on paper in order to feel appreciated. But, there are a few names that I want to put on paper.

I'd like to thank my daughter, Tamirah for the patience and understanding. There were times when I had to break promises and had to cancel activities at the last minute. You never complained (at least not out loud) about any of the compromises that occurred. I love you, pumpkin.

I want to thank Carlton, who never doubted that I could do this. Thank you for giving me the space and time I needed to write without hassle. You always encouraged me—I love you. Next to Tamirah, you are my biggest supporter and fan.

I'd like to thank my mom, Diane Goode, for supporting me when I told her that I was using my life savings to self-publish my book.

Then there are my sisters. Felecia—Much love to you for being a stepmom to Tamirah. If it weren't for you doing those activities that I couldn't, there wouldn't be a book.

Shakirah—you've motivated me to stay focused. Thanks for listening and helping me escape every now and then. And thank you for going 'comma crazy'!!

No, I did not forget about my niece and nephew. Zanasea and Al-Fuquan, I love you guys!

Hakiem, thank you for being my friend. No matter what, you always come when I need you. Thanks for having my back (always in all ways). Luv Ya!

Hey Endy Greene! They say people come into your life for a reason or a season. It's obvious that you're here for a reason. I've figured out that reason. You are here to keep me from complaining. You help me to understand that it could be worse. Thank you for passing down your knowledge and life experiences for me to learn from. Best of luck with your *Decisions* project!

I'd like to give a very special thanks to Terri (smooth) Smith, Sadiq Smith and Darryl Gwaltney for that *'last minute assistance'* you provided. You are lifesavers!

I'd like to thank everyone who read and re-read and then read my book again at my request. I didn't forget about the family and friends who helped with the little things. You know who you are. I hope I've done a good job in making you all feel appreciated. For the support and encouraging words, I thank all of you. And remember, if your name isn't here, it doesn't mean I love and appreciate you any less.

Last but not least, my grandmother Ms. Delores Stokes. You were my first example of a strong black woman. I love you. Thanks!

Chapter 1

I just can't stop thinking about last night. I keep having flash-backs of my evening with Tarik. Tarik and I have been dating for six years. We met the summer of 1994. I was a senior at Hampton University. I was home for summer vacation. I was going to my girl Simone's house for our annual block party BBQ. I stopped for a red light on Newark Ave, in Elizabeth, NJ. He pulled up right beside me and asked if I would pull over so he could talk to me. As I sped off on the green light I yelled, "Now is not a good time, I'm in a hurry!" I'm not going to lie to y'all, I noticed him about two blocks ago. He was what I called *foine*. He had the most beautiful set of bedroom eyes I'd ever seen in my life and he was the complexion of butter almonds. I really don't know why those words came from my mouth but they did and I regretted them as soon as they left my tongue. I arrived at Simone's twenty minutes later. I parked about a block away from her house. I got out of my car and started fixing my clothes. I was wearing a jean mini-skirt with a jean belly shirt that tied in the front. I carefully chose that outfit because I am really proud of my legs and I wanted to show them off today. I looked into my passenger side window to sneak a peak at my hair. I had a swoop ponytail thing going and it was looking fierce. I went in the yard and started greeting friends that I went to high school with. I saw Simone on the grill and went over to kick it with her. I told her about the *foine* guy that I just let get away and she called me every fool in the book. I went inside the house to go to the bathroom and when I came out, I walked dead smack into Mr. *Foine*. He looked at me and smiled. "Hmmmm... We meet again," he said as he grabbed my hands. We began talking and we have been inseparable ever since.

We celebrated seven years together last night. Tarik took me out to one of my favorite soul food restaurants, Sylvia's (in Manhattan). I ordered the smothered fried chicken with potato salad and collard greens and a piece of sweet potato corn bread. Tarik ordered the beef BBQ ribs with macaroni and cheese, potato salad, and corn bread. I was eating that chicken as if I were at home with gravy running all down my fingers. I looked up and Tarik was staring directly into my eyes. I paused from my food and asked him why he had that look in his eyes. He just smiled at me and said that I had never looked more beautiful to him. I smiled back. He then called the waiter to ask for a bottle of White Zinfandel (which is my choice of wine). The waiter returned with the bottle inside an ice bucket and two long stemmed glasses. He filled the glasses with wine while I continued to stare at Tarik like I was a love- struck puppy. The waiter left and Tarik passed me a glass of wine. We toasted to us and I continued to eat and drink the wine. When I got down to the last sip of wine, I noticed that there was something sparkling in my glass. I looked up at Tarik because I knew it had to be some kind of mistake. He smiled at me and then got down beside me on one knee and took my hand. "Tricia, will you marry me?" I was stunned. He removed the glass from my hand took the ring out and placed it on my finger then smiled up at me. I stooped down on the floor right along with him and sang, yes and planted kisses all over his face as if he were a baby. We regained our composure and sat back down. People were staring at us like we were crazy. After all of the excitement, I was no longer in the mood to eat anything. Tarik paid the bill then we left. Needless to say, we went home and fucked like two rabbits in heat. This was the first time in a long while we actually got kinky. I mean Tarik had me in positions that I had forgotten about. He started with some simple foreplay. He began by kissing and rubbing my breast. This led to him licking me from head to toe. Ladies, when I say head to toe, I kid you not. He started at my forehead and slowly moved down to my neck and so on. When he got to my middle spot, I thought I would cum before he even put his tongue on it. As he kissed my inner thighs, he played with my very hard nipples. He jumped off the bed to get a bowl of fruit from the kitchen. He took a plum and put it in my mouth for me to bite. I did and it was so sweet that juice ran down my face, he licked the excess juice from my face then he took a bite. He rubbed the plum on my left breast and then sucked off the juice. He then slid the plum down to my pussy and squeezed juice all over it. It felt so good when the juice started running down my ass. Tarik began to slowly lick and suck my pussy like it was the last meal. I began to moan and fuck his face. I started pumping his face like it was his dick inside of me. After I came, Tarik got up to stick his dick inside of me but I stopped him and laid him on the bed. *Momma went to work.* I poured some chocolate syrup on his dick and began licking like it was a lollipop. I slurped and tried to see how many licks it would take to get to the center. I was sucking so hard and fast, I didn't even notice that he had came inside of my mouth. He stopped and I started to jerk the rest of his juices out of him and began to rub it all over my breast. Tarik turned me on my stomach and stroked me from the back a few times with his fingers and then he dove right in. I don't know how, but he placed my right leg on his shoulder while he fucked me doggy style. I was pumping him back as fast as I could. It felt so good. I must've cum at least three more times. I lay there on my stomach with him

3

still inside of me. We drifted off to sleep. About an hour later, I woke and went to the kitchen to get a glass of cranberry juice. I went back into the bedroom to find Tarik lying on his back stroking himself with a smile. He said, "Round two, you're up." I climbed on top of him and handled my business. Let's just say that I put my man to sleep very satisfied.

This morning, we got up early. We lay in the bed talking. We discussed a wedding date and the colors that we wanted for our wedding. By the way, we're getting married exactly one year from today. About noon, I got up to shower so that I could meet my girl Simone at the gym. Simone and I go way back. We grew up right in the same apartment building.

Simone's family had moved into the same building the summer of 1982 from Virginia. Her family arrived on a bright, sunny, hot day. Trish and two other girls were sitting on a stoop next to the apartment building. Simone walked over to the three girls and asked if they wanted to play double-dutch. "Only if I could be first." Tricia said. The other girls agreed. Simone said in her toughest voice. "No, it's my jump rope so I'm going first."

Trish said, "Well forget you, we're not playing with you. We can play by ourselves. We have enough people. You're the one who needs us to play." Simone rolled her eyes and said, "I don't need y'all to play with me cause I can play by myself."

Tricia's friends left to go home leaving her alone on the stoop. Simone walked right past Tricia and rolled her eyes. Out of nowhere a big dark-skinned boy rode past on his bike and purposely kicked Simone to the ground then laughed at her. She chased the boy down the street until she caught up to him. She reached him and knocked him off the bike and started to whip his ass. Trish ran down the street to break up the fight. She grabbed Simone from behind and told her not to mess with Kareem cause he was the bully on the block. As Trish was getting the two apart, the boy shouted, "I'ma fuck you up, bitch!" Trish let Simone go and both of the girls began whipping on him so badly that Simone's mother came running down the street to break up the fight. The two girls introduced themselves and have been friends ever since.

Chapter 2

This morning as I was doing laundry, I noticed a book of matches in the pocket of the pants that Kareem had on last night. I went to the bedroom and punched his ass on the shoulder. "Get the fuck up Kareem!"

He rolled over. "Yo, what you yelling about?"

I held the matchbook in my hand and said, "You, mutha-fucka!" I took the matchbook and put it right next to his face as he sat up. He looked at it as if he were trying to figure out what it was or where it came from. "This came out of your pants pocket you lying bastard!"

"Simone, what the fuck is you talking about?"

"I'm talking about you being asleep at your parent's house half the damn night. Isn't that what you told me at four o'clock this morning?"

"Simone," he began as he sat up on the bed, "I was asleep at my parents' place! Why would I lie about that?"

"If I was trying to hide something, I would lie too."

"Well I'm not you and I ain't got nuthin' to hide."

"Kareem, how did Marriott Hotel matches get into your pocket?"

"Damn, it's too early for this shit! What matches?"

Simone threw the matches in his face and shouted, "Look don't play fucking games with me. Now who were you with last night?"

"I wasn't with nobody. I told you where I was."

"So that's your story, huh?"

"You know what Simone? I'm so tired of explaining my every move to you. You are either going to trust me or not. We can't be together if you don't trust me. Shit, I trust you!"

"Well Kareem, did we forget that I'm not the one who has a problem being monogamous?"

"Here we go again. That's old news. You said you forgave me for the past. We supposed to be moving forward."

"We are moving forward. We're still together right?"

"Well if that's the case, why do you keep throwing it in my face every chance you get? I asked you if you could put it behind you and you said yes. From what I see, you ain't made no attempts to get past that. Either you forgive me or you don't."

"Kareem, this is not something that I can just sweep under the rug and pretend it never happened."

Kareem swung his legs to the side of the bed.

"Baby, that's not what I'm asking you to do. I need you to move forward. If you can't then maybe I should give you some space and time to think about what you really want."

"What? Are you saying it's over?"

"Simone, I'm not saying it's over but I think we do need some space so you can get yo head together."

"Is this your way of breaking up with me?" Simone asked as she twisted her face into some kind of monster look.

"You're not listening, Simone! I wanna be with you, but I can't if I don't feel like you trust me."

"Kareem, I thought that I could just forget about what happened but it's not that easy. I think you're right. Maybe I do need some time to think things through, but I don't want us to be apart. I promise you that I will deal with this and learn to trust you again but you have to at least meet me halfway."

"That's not my job. You have to wanna trust me. I'm

through proving my love to you. I told you I'm sorry and I meant it but I'm not gonna spend all of my free time up under you so you can keep tags on me."

"That's not what I'm asking, Kareem. I'm just asking that you be a little more patient with me and not give me reasons to doubt you."

"Look Simone, we're not getting anywhere. I'll just go and stay with my parents for a while to give you some time."

"No!" she screamed. "I said I'd be ok. I want you here with me. Baby, I'm sorry for accusing you of anything." Kareem gave her a look of confusion because of the way she screamed the word 'No'.

"You're sure that you'll be able to handle it sweetie?"

"Yeah, I'm sure." Her voice softened.

"Good. Are you meeting Tricia at the gym this morning?"

"Yeah, but I need to do something before I go."

"What's that?" he asked with a smirk on his face.

"I need to *do you* real quick," she responded with a wicked grin.

Kareem and I had two quickies before I jumped in the shower to meet my girl Trish at the gym.

"Tell Trish I said hi," he said as he got under the blanket.

"I will. See you when I get back."

• • •

I arrived at the gym around 1pm, the same time as my girl Trish. We walked inside together. We started off with a dance aerobics class, which lasted about an hour. Next, we went to the treadmill to work on our legs. Finally, we hit the floor mats to work on our abs. Two and a half-hours later, we were on our way to lunch.

"What an intense workout we had today. Simone, you have been unusually quiet. Is there something on your mind?" Tricia asked.

"Well if you insist on being all up in my business, I may as well tell you. Kareem and I got into it again."

"What happened this time?" Tricia asked sarcastically.

"Trish, he had the nerve to come into the house at four in the morning saying that he fell asleep at his parents' house."

"Well, what's wrong with that?"

"I called his parent's house three times last night and his mother told me that she hadn't seen him all day and she didn't even know that he was supposed to come over."

"Damn girl, that's deep!"

"Yeah, I know. So when he got in, I was up waiting for his ass. That's when the shit hit the fan. I asked him where he was and he continued to tell me that he was at his parents' house. I didn't even mention to him that I called there three times looking for him. I let it go last night. He claimed that he just woke up and realized that it was 3:30 in the morning and he wasn't home. So he says that he rushed right home and he was still sleepy."

"Simone, please tell me that eventually you threw it in the air that you knew he wasn't there."

"Will you let me finish? Damn!"

"My bad go ahead." Trish retorted sarcastically.

"I was doing laundry early this morning and I found some Marriott hotel matches in his pants pocket."

"Oh Simone, when are you going to get tired of playing these games with him?" she asked sympathetically.

"Trish, please don't start with me again."

"Simone, I don't mean to start anything, but you can do way better than Kareem."

"And when did you become a relationship expert?"

"Well sweetie," Trish stated calmly. "It doesn't take an expert to figure out when a woman is letting a man dogg her out."

"You see, this is exactly why I don't talk to you anymore. You should concentrate more on being here for me and being my friend instead of judging me."

"Simone?" Trish said in shock. "We have been friends since forever. When did it become such a problem with me expressing my opinion?" Just then, the waitress asked to take their orders. They both ordered chef salads and cold iced teas.

"It's been a problem lately. It seems like you are always putting my relationship with Kareem down."

"I didn't mean it like that. I am just trying to get you to realize that there are other men out here besides Kareem."

"Well Trish, I'm asking you to be my friend. Just be here for me and try not to criticize everything I do just because you don't agree with it. Please?"

Trish stared at Simone in disbelief. But she also saw the pain in her sister friend's eyes. She got up and walked around the table, pulled Simone out of the chair and hugged her. "I'm sorry for causing you pain. I promise from now on to keep my opinions to myself."

"Thank you girl. I just don't know why I'm so crazy over Kareem. I look into those beautiful green eyes, run my fingers through his black naturally wavy hair and I see the man of my dreams. His being 6ft. 8in. doesn't hurt either. He has the perfect body. He's cut in all the right places and don't have any extra inches to pinch in the mid section." Simone looked up and saw Tricia frowning her face in disgust. She laughed and grabbed Tricia's right hand. "Okay. Simone, bring me out of your daydream." Tricia said as she snatched her hand away. Tricia had a smile on her face as she watched Simone compose herself.

"Well," Trish said, "I have some news that will definitely brighten up the mood."

"What's up?"

"Well, Tarik took me out for a special dinner last night."

"Oh, that's right. You two are celebrating seven years together. Congratulations, girl." Simone said with sincerity.

"Well, the exciting part is that he proposed to me during the middle of dinner. "POW!" Trish yelled as she flashed her two-karat diamond rock in Simone's face.

"Ooohhh Trish, let me see. Oh my gosh! This rock is huge girlfriend. I'm so happy for you. Have you guys set a date?"

"Well as a matter of fact, we've decided to get married next year yesterday."

"That gives us enough time to plan the bomb wedding." Simone said with excitement.

"Thanks girl, I was hoping you would say that."

"What else would I say, Trish? You're my dogg and I am going to be by your side every step of the way. That's what friends do."

Trish's eyes began to water. "I'm so glad that we are best friends Simone. You are always here for me and how do I repay you? I put down your relationship with the man you've been in love with for eleven years."

"Oh Trish, stop! You and Kareem have never gotten along. I know that you are only looking out for me." Simone mumbled not believing that Trish was actually apologizing.

"It's true you know. I am only looking out for your best interests." She said as reached out to grab Simone's hand. The waitress returned with their orders and they began to eat and discuss ideas for the wedding.

Chapter 3

I t was Monday morning and Phil was getting ready for work. He was being extremely quiet in the bedroom because he didn't want to wake his wife. She was on vacation from the hospital this week and she didn't need to be up so early. He went to the bathroom to take a shower. Melissa was in the bed tossing and turning. She didn't sleep well without Phil in the bed with her. She heard him in the shower so she decided to surprise him with breakfast before he went to work. She didn't get the chance to cook for him in the mornings since her hours were 7am to 3pm. She had to be at the hospital before Phil had to be up. Melissa has been a registered nurse for seven years. She put her soft cotton robe on and went downstairs to the kitchen to prepare breakfast.

Phil entered the kitchen smiling. "It sure smells good in here. Baby you didn't have to get up to cook. I could have had cereal. You're on vacation, you should be resting," he said while trying to fix his tie.

"I know sweetie, but once I realized you weren't beside me, you know I couldn't sleep. You know I don't have a problem fixing you food. Sit down so we can eat."

"Ok just let me get my shoes."

As soon as Phil walked out of the kitchen, Melissa started fixing the plates. She wanted to sit down to eat as soon as possible because she wanted to discuss an issue with her husband before he went off to work.

"Baby, have you seen my blue shoes? I looked in the bedroom closet but they aren't there."

"Yes. I put them in the hall closet because you hardly wear them."

"Oh, okay."

As Phil sat down to eat, Melissa poured them orange juice. She sat across from Phil wondering how to approach the subject.

"What's on your mind?" Phil asked as he looked up and noticed Melissa playing with her food.

"Well sweetie, I'm wondering what you think about us having a baby."

Phil stared at her for at least two minutes before responding. "Baby, we talked about this a few months ago and we agreed that this isn't the right time." He tried not to sound irritated.

"Yes, I know hon, but that was then and now I think the time is right."

"Why are you so hard up about having a baby, Melissa?"

"I'm not hard up. It's just that I want kids and I know you do too. So why are we waiting? You said we should be married first. We have been married for three years and you continue to say the time isn't right."

"Melissa, let's talk about this when I come in tonight."

"You still have time before you have to leave, let's just discuss as much as we can now," she begged. She knew Phil's opinion about the subject but she needed to convince him to change his mind. She's thirty-two and Phil's forty-five years old and time was not on their side. She did not want to be one of those women on TV being a new mother at forty years old.

"Melissa, it's too early to discuss this. Please, let it go until I get home!" He stated. The look in his eyes told her he wasn't asking; he was telling her that the conversation was over.

"Fine. I'll let it go for now but tonight, no excuses," she said with a halfhearted smile.

"Good. I have to go. I'll see you later," he said as he walked to the door.

"Hon, what time will you be in tonight? I'll have dinner waiting"

"I should be here no later than 6:30pm. If not, I'll call."

"Ok," she said as she kissed him on the cheek.

Melissa gathered the dishes and began washing them. She decided to give the kitchen a thorough cleaning while she was in the mood. After cleaning the kitchen, she went and started on the bathroom in their bedroom. By the time Melissa finished her housework it was 11am. She had nothing planned for the day so she decided she'd go to the mall. She went into the bathroom to run a nice bubble bath. She went down to the kitchen and grabbed a bottle of water. She went back up and entered the bathtub. As the hot water worked its' magic on her body, her mind wandered to when she first met Phil. He was an employee at her parents' clinic. They met at the annual Christmas party that her parents gave for their employees. Melissa really wasn't up for a party that night. Her boyfriend Charles had just dumped her for the third time that year. She vowed that she wouldn't take him back. Charles had a habit of breaking up with her whenever he wanted to fuck someone else. At the party, her father, Dr. Maurice Evans, introduced her to Dr. Phil Monroe. She was twenty-eight at the time. Phil was forty-one. Dr. Evans was not setting his daughter up with Phil. He just needed to talk business with some very important clients and used Phil to sort of baby-sit since she was in such a depressed mood. Melissa and Phil hit it off instantly. She basically fell in love with his very muscular physic. He was built like an NFL running back and stood at 6'2". His complexion is medium brown. He has brown eyes and a baldhead.

Actually, Phil did not look his age. The only facial hair on his face was the peach fuzz under his chin. They began dating shortly after the Christmas party. Her parents were totally against the idea. They did not want their daughter to get involved with a man thirteen years her senior. They had much respect for Phil as an employee but when it came to their daughter, he was not good enough. When Phil proposed to Melissa, her parents boldly objected and told Melissa if she married Phil, they would cut her off financially. Melissa told her parents that she didn't need their money because her future husband would take good care of her. Phil eventually left the Evans' clinic. He opened a small Dr.'s office of his own. They got married less than a year after they met. In Melissa's eyes, it was love at first sight.

The ringing phone startled her and brought her back to the here and now. Since the phone was not in her reach, she let the voicemail pick it up. She examined her body with her hands and noticed that she was gaining weight. Her stomach had grown a small pouch. Her legs had actually gotten bigger and her ass was a little jingly. She made up her mind to make time to start visiting their gym. Phil had a gym built in the basement when Melissa started going out to the gym and returning well after he was home from work. After she washed, she grabbed a towel from the rack and dried her body. She walked into the bedroom to check the message. As soon as she heard his message, she hung up to dial his cell phone.

"Hello?"

"Hey Tarik. I got your message. What's up?" She asked somewhat excited.

"Hey girl. Whatchu doin'?"

"Getting dressed. I'm going to the mall. Why what's up?"

"Well, I have some news for you so why don't I come by your place and we could go to the mall together?"

"Cool."

"Ok, I'll be there in half an hour. Be ready Melissa! You know how you are." He said as he laughed.

"Oh shut up. I'll be ready. See you when you get here."

"Aight, peace."

"Bye" she chuckled as she hung up the phone.

Melissa began to rush around the house to get ready. She knew Tarik was telling the truth. Every time they went someplace together, he'd end up waiting for her at least an hour. This time she was going to be on time because she was curious as to what he had to tell her.

Melissa and Tarik have been friends since they were freshmen in high school. Melissa was dating Tarik's friend Mark back then. Tarik is the one who approached her and asked if she would go out with Mark. She politely told him that she didn't date guys who didn't introduce themselves. Tarik started to explain how shy Mark was but Melissa turned her back and walked away. Tarik stood there dumbfounded. The next day at school, Mark walked up to Melissa and said that he liked her style. Melissa and Mark started dating shortly afterwards. Tarik became the person she would confide in whenever Mark did her wrong. They have remained best friends over the years.

Beep beep. "Melissa, get yo yellow ass out here." She walked to the window of her bedroom and yelled, "I'm on my way, give me two seconds." She gathered her purse, keys, and cell phone and headed out the door. She got in the car, flipped the passenger mirror down and unwrapped her hair. It hung down to the middle of her back with a nice bounce and swing to it.

"Damn girl, you were supposed to be ready. That includes your hair."

"Shut up, Tarik! At least you didn't have to wait this time." She said as she continued to fix her hair.

"It's about damn time, too. This is the first time since I've known you that I didn't have to wait on you. What's up with that?"

"Well you did say you have something to tell me and I didn't want to be in suspense too much longer. So what's up?"

"Well," he said as he sped off into the traffic, "I proposed to Tricia last Friday." He smiled.

"Stop! For real? Oooohh, I'm so happy for you guys. Wait, she did accept right?"

"Of course she did!" Tarik blushed.

"Congratulations Tarik! When am I going to meet this Trish? I can't believe that you guys have been dating for seven years and we've only met briefly at my wedding."

"Girl, you're never gonna change are you?" Tarik asked as Melissa talked a mile a minute.

"No. And you should be used to it. You know talking is one of my favorite hobbies."

There's another reason I wanted to come with you to the mall," he said.

"Yeah, I knew it was something else because as long as we've been friends, you've only come to the mall with me twice. And the last time, you said that you'd never come back with me again." She laughed at the memory.

"Are you going to be long Melissa?" He asked as he pulled into the parking lot.

"No."

"Are you sure because you know how women are and you my dear, are worse than every woman that I know."

"Yes, I'm sure, I have to be home in time to cook dinner for Phil tonight."

Tarik smirked, "You still treating that nicca like he's the man, huh?

"Tarik, it's been three years since my wedding. Please let go of the past. I know that you don't like Phil because he's hit

17

me before. He swore he'd never do it again and he hasn't in over three years."

"Well, I still don't like the idea of anyone putting their hands on you. What gives him the right to hit you? You are not his child!"

"Hey, this is supposed to be a happy day for you, so let's not ruin it by talking about the past."

"Yeah, you're right. But if that nicca ever put his hands on you again, it will be hell to pay. Now, are you ready to get this shopping spree started?"

"Yep." They got out of the car and entered the mall through Bloomingdale's. While walking through the mall, Tarik wondered how in the hell he was going to tell Melissa that his bride to be doesn't like the idea that his best friend is a woman.

He told Tricia about Melissa about three months after they first started dating. Tricia told him that she wouldn't be the second female in his life. She broke off the relationship after Tarik told her that he would not choose. He tried to convince Tricia that Melissa was a platonic friend and nothing more. She wouldn't hear it. He was miserable without her. He had fell hard for Trish in the three months that they'd been dating. He told her that he talked to Melissa and that she understood why he had to redefine their relationship.

"Tarik? Hello? You never did answer my question." Melissa sang.

"What was that?"

"When am I going to formerly meet Tricia?"

"Ok. Melissa there's only one way to say this and that's straight out."

"Say what?" Melissa asked as she pulled Tarik into the Macys dept. store. She went directly to the shoe section.

"Tricia doesn't know that we are still friends. There, I've said it."

"What did you just say?" she asked in disbelief.

"Well, she's under the impression that men and women can't have platonic relationships."

"Did you explain the nature of our relationship to her?"

"I tried but she had a bad experience with an ex-boyfriend and she was not about to go through the same shit again."

"So, that was the end of it? You didn't try harder to defend our relationship? You just let it go and decided we'd be undercover friends?" she asked annoyed.

"No Lissa, it wasn't like that."

Melissa began to raise her voice. "Well, how the hell was it?"

"Will you lower your voice and calm down?" He asked as he pulled her out into the hall of the mall. He walked her down to a nearby bench where they sat and tried to discuss the situation rationally.

"Tarik, I can't believe that you would break our pact. You know, no one can come between our friendship. This was the one thing that you and I were to have forever. Remember? Well thank you for dissing me for a bitch you hardly knew."

"Aight, bring it down a notch Melissa. Don't start calling my fiancé names. Just give me a chance to explain why it went down like this."

"Tarik," she smiled, "It's not necessary that you try to explain anything to me. Just know that you are fixing a lie that you told to your *fiancé*."

"What the hell does that mean?" he raised his voice a notch. Melissa started moving her head side to side and rolling her neck. "Oh no! Don't you dare try that reverse psychology shit with me! You came to me and told me some fucked up shit and you want me to be calm about it? Well you know me better than that."

"Melissa?" Tarik looked at her with those almond shaped eyes that most women would do anything for.

"Wait, it's my turn. You said what you had to say to me."

She stood from the bench. "You can go home and look your *fiancé* in the eye without that stupid, guilty expression on your face and tell her that you didn't lie to her. You did break our friendship. And you broke it the day you dissed me to her. As far as I'm concerned, you can go to hell. I don't have anything else to say to you." With that said, Melissa walked towards an exit door without looking back.

Tarik stood and called her name before she disappeared in the crowd. "Damn!" He said just loud enough for himself to hear.

Chapter 4

M elissa entered the house at exactly 7:30pm. She walked upstairs to the bedroom and saw Phil lying on his back with his hands locked under his head. She sat on the bed contemplating whether or not she'd tell him what happened between her and Tarik. She decided against it because their dislike for each other was mutual. Phil also believed that men and women couldn't be platonic friends, but he never made it an issue with Melissa because he never saw Tarik as a threat.

"Well that was a great dinner you left for me this evening." Phil said in a very sarcastic tone.

"Phil, I totally forgot about dinner. I'm sorry but I've had a very stressful day." Melissa said as she rubbed her temples. She felt a headache coming.

"Well," he said as he sat upright on the bed.

"What was more important than you being here with dinner like you promised? Better yet, what was it that made you forget to at least leave a note so that I'd know where you were and wouldn't worry?"

"Phil, I was with Tarik today and we just got into a terrible argument."

"You know damn well I don't give a fuck about Tarik! You could have at least called, Melissa."

"I know I should've called Phil, but I just needed to be alone to clear my head and think about things." She answered nervously.

"Before I left for work this morning, you were pressuring me about having a baby. When I come home prepared to discuss it, you're not here." Phil noticed himself yelling. He didn't mean to start tripping about her being out but he was a little pissed that she wasn't considerate enough to call.

"Well Phil," she said as she gathered things for a shower, "There are other things on my mind right now. I mean really, I'm at home all day, I cook dinner every night, I don't go out because you don't approve of my friends and now I need your permission to hang out with my best friend?" She grabbed her robe and went inside the bathroom.

Phil got up from the bed and went in the bathroom behind her. "Who in the hell do you think you are coming in here talking to me like that? Have you lost your damn mind or something?"

"Phil please, can I take a shower, alone? I'm really not in the mood to argue with you right now. I told you that I had a stressful day." She said as she gently led him towards the bathroom door. When she got closer to him, she noticed that Phil had been drinking. The last thing she wanted was to get him upset while he had been drinking.

"Now I know you're crazy, putting your hands on me." Melissa went on and started the shower in hopes that Phil will get the message and leave her alone. She began to undress.

"Melissa, tell me something," he said as he walked up behind her. "Why do you need to take a shower?"

She turned around and faced him. "What do you mean, Phil?" She had to keep her balance because Phil was so close up in her face, she almost fell into the tub.

"I'm talking about you being out with your *friend* and coming home in such a hurry to take a shower. Explain please what that's all about?" His speech was slurred because of the amount of alcohol he'd consumed in the past hour. Melissa stepped to the side of Phil and walked back into their bedroom and slipped into her robe. "Phil, I am not about to justify my reasons for taking a shower. What is wrong with you?" She looked at him with teary eyes. He walked over to her and pushed her down on the bed.

"Phil stop!" she yelled as she tried to get out of his reach. Phil was too fast. He climbed on top of her and snatched the bathrobe off of her body. He lowered his head and tried to kiss her. Melissa turned her head away from him.

"Open your fucking mouth, Melissa!"

"No! Phil, please stop!" She really didn't want to upset him because she knew all too well that Phil would roughly take the sex from her and then beat her some more for fighting him.

"Melissa, if you don't open your mouth, I'ma fuck you up!" He had the same look on his face as the day they got married-when he first hit her. She slowly turned her head back towards Phil and let him have his way with her. Phil started slobbering all over her mouth and nipples. He forced himself inside of her. He pumped her six times and then called her name softly as he was having an orgasm. Phil rolled over to catch his breath while Melissa just lay there and stare at the ceiling. After about five minutes, she got up and started towards the bathroom. "Where do you think you're going?" Phil slurred.

"I'm just going to take a shower," she said without looking back. He leaped off the bed and grabbed her by her left arm. He spun her around and slapped her so hard that she fell on the floor. "Now, the next time I won't be so nice. Get up off the floor and go clean yourself, you look a mess!" Melissa got up off the floor and went into the bathroom. She walked to the mirror and noticed the black and blue bruise forming on the right side of her face. She was glad that she would not have to go to work this week. As she stepped into the running water, she said a silent prayer that Phil was sound asleep when she got out.

Chapter 5

Tarik sat at the kitchen table messing around his breakfast while Tricia talked to him about wedding plans. When she got no response from him, she moved closer to him.

"Tarik, what's the matter with you? You have been a little distant for the past two weeks. Is there something you wanna talk about?"

"Tricia, there is something I need to talk to you about."

"Well what is it, Boo? You know you can talk to me about anything." She said as she took his hands in hers.

"Just promise me that you'll keep an open mind about this and that you'll hear me out?"

"Tarik, please don't do that. Just tell me what it is."

"Well, you remember my friend Melissa?"

"Yeah, what about her?"

"When I told you that I broke ties with her, I lied."

Tricia let go of his hands. She stood and began pacing the kitchen. "What do you mean, you lied?"

"Tricia," he said as he stood to stop her from pacing, "Melissa means too much to me to dismiss her like I told you I did."

"Oh so, she means more to you than I do?"

"No, that's not what I'm saying." He sat back at the table and sighed.

"What the hell are you saying, Tarik? You told me that

you and her were no longer friends. How could you lie to me like that?" She asked as she sat back at the table.

"Tricia, you made me choose between you two. I wanted you so badly I was willing to do and say anything to keep us together."

"And you think by telling me you lied for *us*, I'll forget about the whole thing?"

"I'm not asking you to forget about it, just hear me out Tricia. Please?" She had tears in her eyes when she looked at him. "What the hell can you say to me that's gonna make me feel any better about this situation? I mean really, what else have you lied about? How often do you see her?"

Tarik gestured with his hands for her to calm down and listen. "Ok, it's like this. Melissa knows that you exist. She didn't know that you have a problem with our relationship. We only see each other once in a while. She'd call me at work or on my cell. I'll call her and keep her from calling here. We went out a few times since you and I have been together."

Tricia shook her head side to side the whole time Tarik told his story. "I met with Melissa two weeks ago to tell her about our engagement. As usual, she asked when she was going to get the chance to meet you. I had to tell her everything about how you feel about our friendship. She was pissed when I told her that you didn't think men and women could have platonic relationships. Tricia, I have never seen Melissa like this before. It hurt her more to find out that I didn't defend our friendship to you."

Tricia looked at him like she had just seen a ghost. "Tarik, are you saying that her feelings are more important than mine?"

"Damn! Why you gotta keep going there? It's not about whose feelings are more important. The bottom line is I was dead wrong for lying to you. I'll admit that, but I was also wrong to let you dictate to me who my friends should be." Tricia was stunned. "Melissa and I have been friends for over half of our lives and I will not end our relationship because you're inse-cure with it." Her mouth hung all the way down to the table. "Tarik, let me just understand what just happened. You're say-ing that no matter how I feel, you are going to continue to be in this woman's life? You're still going to be friends with her?"

"Tricia, she's my best friend. We've been through so much to...

She cut him off. "I'm supposed to be your best friend."

"Baby, that's not how I meant it. I'm not going to cut her out of my life. Now you need to get used to the idea of me having a female as a close friend and trust me enough to believe that it's platonic."

"Whoa..." she held her hands up in front of her chest. "You don't sit here and tell me that I'ma get used to shit! I decide what I'll stand for... not you! Now if you wanna keep on seeing this so-called *friend*, then you need to think about how much our relationship means to you."

"Tricia, I'm going to try to make up with Melissa. I'm wor-ried about her and I need you to support me on this. Don't give me an ultimatum. I'm not going to choose between the two of you again. I just wish you would take some time to get to know her. She's a wonderful woman and I'm sure you'll like her." She got up from the table. "Well it looks like you've already made up your mind. But let me ask you something? Why are you telling me this now?" She stood by the window with her arms folded like a child not getting her way. "I'm telling you because I don't want to continue keeping this a secret. We are getting married and I want Melissa to be a part of our lives."

"Well, don't be so sure about that. You lied to me and I need to be sure that I can trust you. You knew how I felt about the situation, yet you lied to me... for over six years." She grabbed her car keys and walked out the door. Tarik sat there and looked at the door.

Chapter 6

T ricia called Simone from her car. "Hello?"
"Tricia?"
"Yeah, it's me. You busy?"
"No, what's up?"
"Meet at Momma's house? I'm on my way there now." She hung up the phone and kept driving.

"Tricia? Hello…" Simone grabbed her keys and headed out the door. As she weaved through traffic, she wondered what had Tricia so pissed.

Tricia parked behind her mama's minivan in the driveway. She used her key to enter the house. "Mama you here?"

Mrs. Hobbs entered the living room from the kitchen. She walked over to give her only baby a hug. "What brings you here baby?"

"I need to talk. Simone's on her way too!"

"Well this must be pretty serious for you to round us all up."

Mrs. Hobbs was a tall brown-skinned woman with a very small waist and big hips. Her hair hung down past her shoulders. She was a widow for the past three years. She met her husband Fred at a high school dance. They both attended the dance without dates. Fred was a tall lanky boy with long feet and hands. He was not the most popular boy in school but that's what made Maryanne Parker interested. Fred approached her just when 'Mickey's Monkey' by Smokey Robinson and the Miracles blasted from the stereo. He asked her for a dance. Since she'd been secretly praying that he would, she accepted his hand for a dance. They danced to three more fast songs nonstop. When the first slow song came on, Fred Hobbs hesitantly stepped back from Maryanne not wanting to give her the wrong impression. She looked at him shyly and asked, "Would you like some punch?" Fred smiled and said, "Lead the way." The two teenagers found a somewhat quiet spot near a corner of the school gym and talked the rest of the night. Four months later, Maryanne Parker discovered that she was pregnant. Fred did the honorable thing and proposed to her. She declined his offer saying that her parents would never let her get married at such a young age. Fred was as confused as ever. He called Maryanne every night to discuss their future. Another two months had passed before Maryanne's mother discovered that her daughter was pregnant. Maryanne was kicked out of her parent's house the same evening. She went crying straight to Fred. He again asked her to marry him. Again, she refused. Fred would not let the mother of his child be homeless so he dropped out of school and took a job with General Motors. Fred and Maryanne found a nice affordable one-bedroom apartment where they would live for the next ten years. When Tricia was eleven years old, her father came home one day and announced that they were moving to their own house. Maryanne was ecstatic. The day they were to move into their new house, Fred again proposed to his woman of eleven years. "Maryanne, I've loved you since our first dance. Please do me the honor of being my wife?" This was the first time Maryanne thought Fred was asking because he loved her and not out of obligation. She was ready to become Mrs. Fred Hobbs.

"Yes Fred, I will be your wife." She smiled at him as she gave him a hug.

"Maryanne, what took you so long to say yes?"

"Well, I just needed to make sure that we were ready. I needed to make sure that a marriage wasn't going to hold you back from your goals."

"Maryanne, you and Tricia are my life. I've been trying to tell you this for years." He said as he kissed her passionately on the mouth.

Mr. and Mrs. Fred Hobbs would stay married for the next thirteen years.

Fred Hobbs had an unexpected fatal heart attack that killed him instantly three years ago.

"Mama it is serious," she said as tears welled in her eyes. "Tarik and I just had a falling out and I don't think we can fix this. There may not be a wedding."

"Girl, what you talking?" *Ding- dong. Ding-dong.*

"I'll get it mama, that's Simone." Tricia opened the door and found Simone standing there with her hand on her pocketbook.

"Who I gotta cut?" She asked as she walked into the house and saw the tears in Tricia's eyes.

"Come on in girl." Tricia stepped back and allowed Simone to embrace her in a much needed sister girlfriend hug.

"Hi moms." Simone said as she walked over to give Mrs. Hobbs a hug. Mrs. Hobbs loved Simone like she was her own child.

"Hey baby. How are you?"

"I'm fine. But right now, I'm trying to find out what's wrong with Tricia."

"I don't know, but I'm ready to find out, too."

"Let's go into the kitchen." Tricia said as she brushed passed the two women. They followed her and took seats at the table.

"Ok baby we're all here, tell us what happened." Mrs.

Hobbs said. Tricia stood by the sink and began sobbing even harder. Mrs. Hobbs got up to help Tricia to one of the chairs at the table. Simone went to the fridge to grab some iced tea. As she poured three glasses, Tricia began to tell her story. She told them everything about what she and Tarik discussed that morning. She explained her feelings about the situation and she also described how Tarik felt. When she finished, Mrs. Hobbs just sat there and stared at her daughter like she was crazy. "Tricia, are you telling me that you are going to break up with the man because of his friends?"

"Mama, it's not like it's just one of the boys he hangs out with, she's a woman."

"So, what's the big deal?" Simone injected.

With much attitude Tricia responded, "The big deal is that I don't like the idea of my man running around with another woman. And you should understand that all too well Mrs. 'I found my man cheating again!' "

"Time out." Mrs. Hobbs said as she held her hands in the 'T' position. "Tricia that was very childish. This is not about Simone and Kareem, it's about you and Tarik. You came to us for help and support. Now we're just trying to understand the problem." Simone stared at Tricia with an icy glare. "I'll just act like you didn't go there since you are pissed to the max." Simone said between clenched teeth. "Simone, I'm sorry." Tricia spoke softly. "I was wrong to even go there. I'm just so pissed with Tarik that I took it out on you. You know they say misery loves company," she smiled at Simone hoping to warm her up.

"Ok. Tricia, you've lost me. Why are you so insecure about Tarik having female friends? You have male friends."

"I know, but that's different."

"Explain how." Mrs. Hobbs interjected.

"Mom, I just think that this woman has other intentions with Tarik."

"Well what has she done to make you think like this?"

"She hasn't actually done anything, I guess. She's just..."

"Tricia," Simone interrupted, "Have you even met this woman?"

"Well no, not exactly."

"What does that mean?" Mrs. Hobbs asked.

"Tarik introduced us at her wedding. We had a brief conversation at the reception."

"She's married and you still have a problem with her and Tarik being friends?" Simone asked.

Tricia just looked down at the table and began to cry again. Mrs. Hobbs drank her iced tea in one gulp and sat the glass on the table. She looked at her daughter in disbelief. "Tricia, you plan on getting married to a man that you don't trust?"

"Mama, I trust Tarik."

"I don't see how. You've spoken to this woman for a brief moment on her wedding day. You didn't even give yourself a chance to get to know her. Why are you so insecure if she hasn't given you any reason to be?"

"Ma, how would you feel if daddy woulda told you that he has a woman that he hangs out with?"

"Tricia, men will be men until the end of time. You can't stop him from being friends with anyone. I can see if he came to you after a few years and announced that he has a new friend. Then you would have reason to suspect that there is something going on. But he's being upfront with you by telling you this and you're telling him that you don't trust him."

"But..."

"Wait, I'm not finished, Tricia. You expect him to accept the fact that you have male friends but you won't even try to accept his female friends. How selfish are you?"

"Tricia, just give the girl a chance. Obviously, he cares a great deal for her if he decided to tell you the truth," Simone added.

"I don't know," Tricia said, "I still can't get over the fact that he lied to me for all these years."

"Well look at it like this," Simone said with a wicked smile. "You keep your friends close but your enemies closer."

"No, no, no! You ladies are missing the point." Mrs. Hobbs said aggravated. "My point is that you need to get to know her before you decide that you don't like her. Just give him the same trust that he gives you when it comes to your friends."

"Well mama, I need some time to think about this. Can I stay here for a couple of days?"

"Tricia, you know you don't have to ask. You can stay here for as long as you like, but I do think you should consider going home to your man and work this thing out."

"I will mama, but I just don't want to face him tonight."

"Well at least call him so that he'll know you're alright."

"Ok, ma."

"Well ladies, I'm going to the attic to finish my cleaning."

"Ok moms, I'll come up before I leave." Simone said.

"Ok mama, see you in a bit."

As Mrs. Hobbs left the kitchen, Simone went to the fridge to pour more iced tea. "Want some?" She asked to Tricia.

"No, I'm fine." She looked at Simone with teary eyes.

"Tricia, what's the real reason you don't want to meet this woman?"

"Simone, I met her at the wedding and she is gorgeous. I just have this gut feeling that there is an attraction between those two."

"Please Tricia, you and I both know that Tarik adores you and would not think about another woman. Consider the fact that he told you about her. He didn't have to do that."

"Yeah, I've been thinking about that. But I don't know about meeting with her trying to be friends."

"Why not? At least you'll know what she's all about."

"True."

"Look girl, I've gotta go. Kareem is taking me to the movies tonight and I still need to run some errands. Are you going to be ok?"

"Yeah girl, I'll be fine. Thank you for coming."

"Please, you know I got your back." Simone went upstairs to say goodbye to Mrs. Hobbs. She came back down the stairs, said bye to Tricia, then left.

• • •

Across town, Kareem was getting his dick sucked by his side chic, Shelly. He sat on the foot of the bed and watched her deep throat his dick several times before he came in her mouth. He pulled her up on the bed, lay her on her stomach and fucked her doggie style.

"Where you going baby?" Shelly asked as Kareem went to shower.

"I told you that I am taking Simone out tonight. I need to get on her good side for a while. I barely got out of the lie I told her a few weeks ago."

"Shit. I'm so tired of sharing you with another woman."

"Shelly, don't start. You knew about her way before we started fucking. You knew she was my main lady, so don't act like I promised you something more than this." He walked to the bathroom and turned on the shower. Shelly followed. "Yeah, but things have been going great between us. Why can't we take this to the next level?"

"Like I told you in the beginning, I'm not leaving Simone for you or anyone else."

"So why bother cheating at all?"

"It's bitches like you who allow me to cheat so you need to look at yourself for answers." He closed the door and left her standing there looking hurt.

Kareem hadn't meant to hurt Shelly's feelings. But she was getting too serious for him lately. She knew she was just a booty call and now she wants to make it more than what it is. When he came out of the bathroom, Shelly was bending over with her back to him doing some stretches. He walked over to her. "You think you slick don't you? Looks like I'ma hafta think of another lie cause you just got my undivided attention." He said as he stroked himself and carried her to the bed.

Chapter 7

M elissa's vacation was practically over. She'd have to return to work in two days. She got out of bed and went to the kitchen. She noticed a gift wrapped box on the countertop. She wasn't surprised. Phil had been buying her expensive gifts all week. It was his way of apologizing for hitting her. She opened the box and found a diamond tennis bracelet. Melissa put it on and began to fix herself breakfast.

Ring ring ring. "Hello?"

"Hey Melissa, its Tarik."

"What is it, Tarik?" She asked irritated.

"Melissa don't hang up. I want to apologize to you. I was dead wrong and I need you to accept my apology."

"What you need is your *fiancé*, not my friendship."

"'Lissa give me a break, I am trying."

"Tarik, just let it go. I did. Apparently our friendship doesn't mean as much to you as it does to me."

"I would like for you and Tricia to meet formerly."

"And how are you going to get her to agree to this?"

"Just leave that part to me. The four of us will have dinner?" It was more of a statement than a question.

"Fine Tarik, we'll do dinner. I'll call you."

"Cool, that'll work. Thanks Melissa. We'll see y'all."

"Bye." She hung up.

Melissa didn't know what to think. She knew that she

needed Tarik in her life. He's the brother she never had. Her main concern was how she was going to get Phil to agree to dinner with Tarik and Tricia. Melissa finished breakfast and went to the bedroom mirror to look at the bruises on her face. The swelling had gone down but there was still a blue ring around her eye. She gathered clothes and went to the shower.

When Phil arrived home that evening he handed Melissa another gift box. She hesitantly took the box. "Thank you. Phil, you don't have to keep buying me gifts."

"Yes I do baby. You deserve all this and then some. I'm really sorry for hitting you. Melissa, I love you so much."

"I love you too. You promised me that you'd never hit me again."

"I know baby but I was drunk. You know how I get when I drink. I lose all control."

"Phil, look at me!" She sobbed. "I have to go to work Monday morning looking like a punching bag. Do you know how embarrassing this is?" she asked pointing to her face.

"Lissa, I'm sorry. It won't happen again. I swear. Please forgive me sweetie?"

She looked down and shook her head back and forth. "I forgive you Phil, but this can not happen again!" She hated the fact that she was so weak when it came to her husband. No matter what Phil did, she'd always find it in her heart to forgive him. She loved him more than she loved herself at times. "So open your gift baby." She began unwrapping the box. She pulled out the matching anklet to the tennis bracelet. "Oh my goodness! This is beautiful."

"Not as beautiful as you."

"I love them. Thank you."

"How about you go get dressed and I'll take you out to dinner?"

"Can we go to Red Lobster or something? I really don't want people to see my face."

"Anything you want, sweetheart."

"Ok. Just give me about half an hour."

In the car they decided that they would go to Houlahan's. Melissa enjoyed being able to dress down. Every time she and Phil went out, they had to dress to impress. They were usually entertaining some of Phil's business associates.

"Phil, Tarik wants me to finally meet Tricia."

"That's great sweetie," he said as he watched the basketball game on the big screen T.V. in the restaurant.

"He suggested that the four of us get together for dinner."

"If that's what you want Lissa, I'll do it."

"Are you serious? She asked shocked.

"Yes, I'm serious. If that's what'll make you happy, then I'm all for it."

"Thank you, baby. I really appreciate you doing this."

"When is this supposed to happen?"

"I don't know. I'll have to set it up."

"Just let me know when and where." Melissa didn't think it was going to be this easy to convince Phil to have dinner with them.

They finished their meal and took a drive to the pier in Jersey City where they walked the Boardwalk and talked for two hours. Afterwards, they went home and made love for the rest of the night.

Chapter 8

Kareem walked in the apartment at 2:00am. Simone was sitting on the bed reading a book. Kareem walked over and kissed her on the cheek. "Hey baby."

"Hey baby my ass!"

"Simone, I know you're mad but I..."

"Mad. You think I'm mad, Kareem? No. I'm not mad. I'm pissed the fuck off!" She got out of the bed and went over to him. She began sniffing his collar. "Yo, what the hell you doing?'

"I'm just trying to see if you had the decency to wash her scent off before crawling back to me."

"Simone, please don't start this shit again."

"Kareem, where were you?"

"Simone, I went to the bar with some of the guys from work and I lost track of time."

"Why didn't you answer your cell phone?"

"I must have forgotten to turn it on when I got off work."

"Before you left this morning, I reminded you that we had plans."

"I know, and I promise to make it up to you."

"How the fuck do you plan to do that? She asked with her hands on her hips.

"We'll just go next weekend."

"Do you really think that I'm going to wait around for you

to stand me up again? Apparently you fell and bumped your head on the way home."

"Simone baby, why you gotta act like this? I said I'm sorry."

"You damn right you're sorry!" She said as she walked out of the bedroom and slammed the door. *Well at least she won't be bitching with me all night* Kareem thought. No sooner than the thought left his mind, Simone opened the door and calmly said, "I hope you don't think that you're gonna come in here and sleep in this bed with me. Go back to the bitch you was with half the night." Kareem knew not to push it so he went to the living room and slept on the sofa.

• • •

"Hello?"

"Hey, it's me."

"You at your moms?"

"Yeah."

"Tricia are you just going to walk out of the house every time we have an argument or disagreement?"

"Tarik, I'm sorry I walked out on you but I needed time to think."

"So…now what?"

"I'm going to stay here tonight and I'll be home after work tomorrow."

"Why won't you just come home so we can work this thing out?"

"Boo, I promise that tomorrow we can sit and talk this thing through. I still need some time to think."

"Alright Tricia, if that's what you want."

She hung up the phone and lay in bed thinking about her future. She has been in love with Tarik since their first date. She is all prepared to marry him. The only thing left was for her to prepare to meet his 'friend'. Maybe Simone was right about keeping your enemies closer.

Chapter 9

M elissa had made plans for her and Phil to meet Tarik and Tricia at the Outback Steakhouse on Route 10. She was nervous as hell. She hadn't spoken to Tarik once since their conversation about the dinner plans. She was trying to find something comfortable to wear. She didn't know what to expect with Tricia not liking her and all. "Phil sweetie, what are you going to wear?" She yelled into the bathroom. He was shaving his mustache and beard. He came out and stood in the doorway. "Melissa there is a medical convention that starts tomorrow and I'm not going to be able to make it to dinner with you guys. I'm leaving tonight."

"What?"

"Well, I just found out about it this morning."

"Why are you just now saying something about it, Phil?"

"I didn't know how to tell you. I know how excited you were about this evening and I was trying to find the right time to mention it."

"Well an hour before we're supposed to be there does not qualify as the right time." She said agitated.

"Melissa, don't be upset. This is work and I have to be there."

"You know Phil, it's not about you going because if you have to go then you have to go. It's about you being considerate enough to tell me sooner. How do you think I'll feel sitting there alone? What am I supposed to tell them?"

"You'll tell them the truth. I couldn't make it. Let's schedule another meeting where they can come over here for drinks or something."

"Phil, you are so full of shit. You probably knew about this trip since the night I told you about the dinner."

"Melissa," he said as he began packing his suitcase.

"I'm not going to argue with you about it. I can't go and that's the end of it!"

She looked at Phil and lost the battle of trying to hold her tears. She sat on the bed and debated about calling Tarik to cancel. She watched Phil pack undergarments and socks. She knew she didn't want to sit around the house alone so she decided to finish getting dressed. "Where are you going Phil?"

"I'll be in Atlanta for the next five days. As always, I'll leave my flight information and hotel number by the phone in the kitchen."

"Whatever," she answered and walked in the bathroom. When she finished getting dressed, she grabbed her cell phone and car keys then left.

Phil just watched her go. He never had any intentions of going to dinner with Melissa and her friends. She knew he and Tarik didn't get along. He just couldn't understand why she insisted that they become friends. Phil loved Melissa as best as he could. He provided for her in every way possible. She didn't want for anything. She insisted on having a job so that she could have her own money. He was fine with her working. It showed him that she could be independent. Phil was beginning to feel that Melissa was not the woman he was meant to marry. He really loved her but she was beginning to get on his last damned nerves about having a child. Phil never wanted children and he only told Melissa that he did because it meant so much to her. He thought that if he kept her busy taking trips and planning business parties for him that she would realize

41

that they had no time for a child. *'Damn, I just have to do what I have to do'.* Phil thought. He called for a car service to take him to the airport. He left the necessary information in the kitchen next to the phone as usual. He left her a note then left.

Chapter 10

M elissa arrived at the restaurant twenty minutes late. She went in the lobby and a waiter greeted her immediately. "Table for one ma'am?"

"No, actually, I'm here to meet the Tarik Hammond dinner party."

"Yes ma'am, they are already seated. Come this way."

"Thank you." she replied as she followed the waiter to the table. He pulled out her chair and introduced himself as Dorian and said he'd be back to take their orders shortly.

As soon as their waiter left, Tarik stood to give Melissa a hug.

"Hey Lissa, this is my fiancé, Tricia Hobbs. Tricia, this is my dear friend Melissa Monroe." Tricia stood and shook Melissa's hand.

"Nice to meet you Tricia." She smiled.

"Is Phil parking the car?" Tarik asked.

"No. Unfortunately, he's not going to make it. He had to leave tonight to go to a medical convention."

"Oh, I'm sorry to have missed the chance to meet him." Tricia said. "I'm sure the three of us will have a good time anyway."

"Yeah." Tarik said nervously. He wasn't sure what to make of Tricia. They talked about this dinner for two days and she seemed okay with the idea of meeting Melissa. But she was just too calm about the subject every since she came back home from her mom's place.

Melissa took her napkin and placed it in her lap. She was feeling a little awkward just sitting there. The waiter returned and everyone placed their orders. Tarik was the first to break the silence. "Melissa, I just want to start by saying that I'm sorry for not explaining to you in the beginning how Tricia felt about our relationship."

"Wait Tarik, let me interrupt for a minute," Tricia said. "I want to say something to Melissa also. I apologize for pre-judging you. I never should have put Tarik in the position of choosing between us. It's obvious that he cares a great deal for you and I should have respected that. I just needed to get that off my chest. I don't want you to feel uncomfortable." Tarik just looked at his woman in amazement.

"Well I'm glad you feel this way Tricia because I would like nothing more than to get to know the woman in Tarik's life. I hope that we can become friends in time."

"Me too," Tricia smiled.

"So, how are the wedding plans coming along?"

"We're managing. You know how men are. We women make the decisions and the men agree to anything." Tricia said. The waiter returned with their meals and they began to eat. Afterwards, they ordered drinks and continued talking.

"If you guys need any help with the wedding, please let me know." Melissa offered.

"Thank you Melissa, we'll keep that in mind," Tricia said.

"Well ladies if you'll excuse me for a moment." Tarik got up to go to the restroom after he finished his meal.

"Melissa, how about you and I go out without Tarik some-time. We can go to the club or something."

"That sounds great. Just let me know when and I'll be there."

"Cool. I just feel like we can get to know each other on

the sista to sista tip without Tarik around."

"I feel you girl." She hushed up quickly when she saw Tarik returning.

"So Melissa, what kind of doctor is your husband?"

"He practices internal medicine." At the mentioning of Phil, Tarik became irritated and said that it was getting late. He and Tricia walked Melissa to her car with promises to do this again soon. "Melissa, I'll call you some time next week."

"Ok guys and thanks for everything. Luv ya." She kissed Tarik on the cheek and got in her car.

"Ok. Be careful girl," said Tricia.

"Luv ya back," Tarik yelled. He got in the passenger side of his truck.

"She really is nice." Tricia said as she fastened her seatbelt.

"I told you she was good people. You just needed to get to know her."

"Well I plan on doing just that. We've made plans to get together for a night out."

"I'm glad. Thank you Boo for everything that you're doing."

"Tarik, I meant what I said. I really feel stupid about my actions. I should have gotten to know her instead of letting my insecurities get the best of me."

"Insecurities? Boo you have nothing to be insecure about. I love you and there isn't another woman out here that I'd rather spend the rest of my life with. I'm off the market. I am yours completely." Tarik held her hand for the rest of the ride home.

Phil felt bad about what he'd done to his wife tonight. He knew Melissa was looking forward to meeting Tarik's fiancé. There were more important things on his mind tonight. He sat in his hotel suite trying to think of a reason not to go through with the appointment he made with the specialist. He couldn't. He picked up the phone to call Melissa but just as quickly put it back in its cradle. He had a big day tomorrow. He decided to take a shower and go to bed. He'd call Melissa in the morning.

Chapter 11

K areem stayed at home with Simone for a week. He'd get up and try to make love to her before he went to work. She rejected his advances three days in a row. As he was getting dressed he thought about all he'd put Simone through. He knew that she loved him with all of her heart. He just couldn't seem to be faithful to her. She'd defended him to her family and friends on numerous occasions. He also knew that one day she'd move on without him. Kareem has been cheating on Simone for the past eight years. She'd caught him with at least ten different women over the years. Each time he'd given her a speech declaring his undying love for her and told her that it would never happen again. He would spend quality time with her and treat her like a queen for a few weeks. He knew that Simone wanted him to marry her. He also knew that she would put up with any amount of his bullshit in order to keep him. That's the reason why he didn't have a problem cheating on her. She wasn't enough of a challenge for him. She would let him get away with too much. Kareem decided on one more attempt to have sex with Simone before he went to work. He went over to the bed where she was laying and bent down to kiss her. She kept her eyes closed pretending to be asleep. He nibbled in her ear and started rubbing on her breasts. She had this tingling feeling between her legs. She really wanted to reject him again but she couldn't ignore her body. She began to kiss him back and to rub between his legs. Simone pulled Kareem on the bed with her and started to undo his pants. He didn't think that she would give in but he went with the flow. He put his face underneath the blanket and began sucking below her belly button. She scratched his back and moaned until she reached her orgasm. Kareem came up from below and put his penis in her face. She pushed him aside and he fell hard on the bed. She got on top of him and started to ride his penis. She rocked back and forth until Kareem pulled her hair and sat up to suck her breasts. A few minutes later, he climaxed. She got up from the bed and grabbed her robe. While walking to the bathroom she said very calmly, "Don't ever put your dick in my face again if you wanna keep it!" Kareem sat up on the bed exhausted and waited for Simone to come out of the bathroom. The minute she came out he went in to wash up. Afterwards, he kissed Simone goodbye and went to work thirty minutes late.

Simone called Tricia to see if she wanted to get together for drinks after work to discuss wedding plans. *Ring, ring*
"Hello."
"Hey bitch. What up?"
"What's up, girl?"
"Are you up to having some drinks after work?"
"Yeah. Same spot?"
"Yep."
"A'ight, see you then." Simone then called the accounting firm and told her boss that she wouldn't be in. She lied and said that she had a stomach virus. She just needed to take some time and think about her life. She couldn't figure out how she and Kareem grew so far apart. She loved him unconditionally but she was beginning to give some thought to what Tricia was always saying. *There's more to life than Kareem.* Simone decided to go visit with Moms today. She needed someone to

talk to and she could not talk to Tricia. Tricia just couldn't seem to understand that she was totally in love with Kareem and was determined to do everything in her power to make it work.

Simone rang the doorbell twice. Mrs. Hobbs looked through the peephole and opened the door. "Hey baby. What are you doing here? Is everything okay?"

"Yeah moms, everything is fine." Simone said as she walked inside the house. "I just need to talk."

"Well, why didn't you use your key?"

"Because I knew you weren't expecting me. I'm sorry I didn't call first."

"Chile hush. Since when do you need to call before you come? If that were the case, you wouldn't have a key."

Simone smiled and took off her jacket. She took a seat on the lazy boy chair that she'd claimed when she and Tricia were in high school. "Moms, I need some advise."

"Is Tricia on her way?" asked Mrs. Hobbs.

"No. I'm getting together with her after work to discuss wedding plans."

"So what's wrong, Chile?"

"Well it's the same ole drama but a different day."

"Kareem?"

"Of course."

"Moms, I don't know what to do about him."

"Sure you do," said Mrs. Hobbs. "You just want someone to tell you what to do and you know that I'm not going to do that."

"But mom I really need some guidance on this one. I came to you because Tricia doesn't understand what I'm going through. I don't plan on discussing this with her."

"Well why don't you start by telling me the problem."

"It's just that he's being extremely disrespectful to me." Simone said while looking at the floor.

"How so?"

"Well, Kareem has been spending more and more time away from me saying that he's with his friends."

"And you don't believe him?" asked Mrs. Hobbs.

"Not really. Ever since the last time I caught Kareem with another woman, I've had a hard time trusting him."

"Simone you and I both know that no relationship can survive without trust."

"I know. I just don't know how to trust him again."

"Maybe you should ask yourself if you want to trust him again."

"What do you mean?" Simone asked with concern.

"I mean that Kareem has allowed you to catch him in many compromising situations over the years. You know, when men cheat they don't necessarily have to get caught. Kareem has gotten busted repeatedly. Have you ever asked yourself why?"

"Dang mom, you sound like Tricia." Simone smiled.

"I'm serious. Just think about it. Do you think that you're worth more than what Kareem is giving you?"

"Yeah, sometimes."

"Are you saying that you deserve to be dogged out and disrespected?" Mrs. Hobbs asked.

"No. That's not what I think. I think he'll change eventually."

"And are you willing to wait for him to change?" Simone just looked at Mrs. Hobbs with a dumb expression. "Simone you've been involved with Kareem for damn near twelve years. What do you want from him?"

"I want us to settle down and get married and maybe have some children." Simone said with a smile on her face.

Mrs. Hobbs didn't know whether to slap some sense into Simone or to give her a hug for being so simple. "Simone baby, is this the man that you want to spend the rest of your life with?"

"He's the only man I have ever loved. We have so much history together. I can't let it all go just like that. Kareem is the one who helped me to deal with my mom's death. If it weren't for him, I'd be dead too."

"Well that's a choice you have to make. But you need to understand that you cannot change any man. If you choose to wait around for Kareem to get his shit together, then you'll have to accept whatever it is he's dishing out to you. What's the use of complaining if you're just going to continue to be with him?"

"Moms, you are you making it seem like I'm stupid?"

Mrs. Hobbs had a blank expression on her face. "If it sounds stupid to you, then you need to ask yourself why. You have a lot to think about. Don't think that you owe him something for being there for you after your mom passed on. It was his job as your man to be there for you. Now, I'm going to clean the kitchen. You just sit here and let my words of wisdom marinate in your head." Mrs. Hobbs said as she walked through the dining room into the kitchen.

Simone sat there in her thoughts for at least two hours. She was sitting on the chair crying when Mrs. Hobbs returned.

"Simone, why are you crying?"

"I just feel so stupid for putting up with his shit for all these years. I heard everything you said. I've been listening when Tricia talk to me, but I just can't bring myself to leave him alone Moms."

"It's ok chile. When you're ready, you'll leave and not a minute sooner. No one can tell you when you've had enough. Only you can determine that."

"Thanks for not judging me." Simone said as she hugged Mrs. Hobbs.

"Hush chile. You know you are the second child that I never could have. I love you baby and I'm always here for you."

With that said, Simone left.

Chapter 12

Tricia sat at the bar and waited for Simone. She ordered an absolute with cranberry juice. She looked divine in her black pantsuit. She stood at five seven and was the color of brown sugar. Her hair hung just below her ears. She had slanted eyes and thick lips. As soon as the bartender arrived with her drink, her cell phone rang. *This better not be Simone calling to cancel, she thought.* "Hello?"

"Tricia?"

"Yeah, who's this?"

"It's Melissa. How are you?"

"Oh hey girl. I'm fine what's up?" Tricia asked.

"Are you busy tonight?"

"Well my girl Simone is meeting me for drinks in a few."

"Oh. Okay. How about we do the bond thing and go out tomorrow."

"Tomorrow's fine with me. But here comes Simone so I really have to go. I'll call you in the morning."

"Ok. See ya." Melissa said disappointedly. She didn't feel like sitting in the house again. She'd try one more friend and then call it a night.

Simone made her way through the crowd. She turned down several offers for drinks. Simone was what most people called dark and lovely. Her skin was the color of dark chocolate. She

52

had light brown eyes and was five foot ten inches with a shoulder length bob haircut. She had curves in just the right places and she walked with all the confidence in the world. She reached the bar and saw Tricia ending a call. "What up girlie?" Simone asked. "Ain't nothing. Same shit different day." Tricia said and laughed.

"So girl, tell me how did dinner with Melissa and her husband go?" Simone asked anxiously.

"It went well. I finally had the chance to formerly meet her but her husband didn't show. He had some kind of medical conference to attend." Tricia said.

"So her husband is a doctor?"

"Yeah. As a matter of fact, that was her on the phone. We're going to the club tomorrow. Wanna come with us?"

"No. That's ok I'll go the next time. You two should go and get to know each other." Simone said.

"Simone she's really nice. I totally misjudged her. I am really looking forward to hanging out with her."

"See, I told you. For all you knew this girl could be a diva like us."

"Very funny. Are you sure you won't join us?"

"Nah. I'm staying in tomorrow."

Simone suggested that they get started on the invitation list. Tricia knew that she and Simone knew the same people so she suggested that they start with the food. "Well whatchu think we should feed these folks?" Tricia asked.

"That's up to you girl. It's your day. What would you like to eat?" Simone asked as she flagged the bartender.

"No. I really don't care. I'm just content with walking down the aisle and becoming Mrs. Tarik Hammond." She smiled.

"I hear you girlfriend but you really need to decide what the menu's gonna look like cause we need to get a caterer in a hurry."

"How 'bout we do the soul food thing?" She said with a

huge grin.

"Oh, so you do remember our old wedding plans." Simone asked with the same grin on her face. When they were children, they'd always plan to have a double wedding with soul food to eat. And they always said that mama Hobbs would do all the cooking since she was the best cook on the East Coast, according to close friends and family. "How could I forget?" Tricia asked.

"Well you're the only one getting married but you still wanna do it?"

"If you're ok with it." Tricia said.

"Girl please! It's your day. Whatever you want." Simone smiled.

They went over a few more things and agreed that they were going to get together next weekend at Mama Hobbs' house to discuss more details.

Chapter 13

P hil returned from Atlanta exactly as planned. Melissa was still at work when he entered their house. He was glad to have the time alone. Although he missed her, he really wasn't up to her nagging about his trip. Phil went straight to their bedroom to take a shower. He realized that Melissa would be home in half an hour. He planned on being asleep when she arrived. He went to unpack his suitcase. He took his briefcase and sat it on the bed. He opened it and removed a gold necklace with an angel charm and placed it on the nightstand. This was the gift he'd brought for Melissa. Melissa came home at her usual time. She went upstairs to take a shower and noticed Phil sound asleep in the bed. *He must have had an exhausting trip.* She thought. She tiptoed around the room so she wouldn't wake him. She took her shower and decided to start dinner before she and Tricia went out. She didn't know what kind of mood her husband was in so she decided to tell him as soon as he woke. Surprisingly, Phil didn't wake up on his own. She had to awaken him for dinner. When he sat up on the bed, she kissed him on the mouth seductively and asked, "How was the trip?" "Same as usual," he replied. He reached over on the nightstand and grabbed her necklace and charm. "Look what I brought back for my baby." He said as he handed it to her.

"Phil, you brought me something?" She smiled knowing

damned well he would bring her something back.

"Of course I did. Have I ever gone anywhere and not bring something back for my baby?"

"Well, thank you sweetie. What's the charm?" She asked while trying to hold it upright.

"That is an angel. I chose that to remind you that you'll always be my angel," he said as he hugged her. "I missed you baby."

"I missed you too."

As they headed down for dinner, Melissa couldn't think of a better time to approach the subject again. As she began fixing their plates, she asked Phil again about starting a family. Phil grew silent. When she joined him at the table, she thought she was hearing things. "Melissa, we can start working on a family."

"What? What changed your mind? When did you decide?" She asked.

"While I was in Atlanta, I realized that I will do anything to make you happy. And if it's a child you want, then a child you'll get." He heard himself say before he could think about his answer.

"Phil, I'm so happy. I wish we could start right now but I have plans tonight." She cringed her face as she spoke because she didn't know how he would react to her going out especially since he just came home.

"Oh yeah? What kind of plans?"

"Well Tricia and I are going out to get to know one another without Tarik." She explained.

"Oh how did the dinner go last weekend?"

"It went well. Tricia and I decided that we could get to know each other if we did the girl thing." She replied.

"Well go ahead and have fun. I won't wait up," he said while eating the stuffed shells that she prepared. Melissa couldn't believe how Phil reacted towards her tonight. Phil is the type of man that needs to have his wife in eyesight at all times. He hardly ever allowed Melissa to go anywhere without him. She didn't know what happened in Atlanta but she liked it a lot. She went upstairs to get dressed. Phil was willing to let Melissa travel to West hell and back if that's what she wanted to do. *Anything to keep from having sex with her tonight.* He thought. Phil would make sure that he'd be asleep when she came home.

Chapter 14

Tricia waited for Melissa to show up at the lounge bar. She showed up a little early to have a drink and mentally prepare for the evening. Tricia was wearing black Capri's and a burgundy halter-top with matching stiletto heels. She sat at the bar and ordered an absolute and cranberry juice. There was a gentleman sitting on the other end of the bar. The man watched Tricia from the moment she walked through the door. He approached her just before her drink arrived. "Is this seat taken?" he asked.

"Actually I am waiting for someone," she replied.

"Do you mind if I buy you a drink and wait with you?"

"Well I just ordered my drink and I'd rather wait alone," she said in an even tone.

"Well if you change your mind, I'm at the other end of the bar," he said and turned away. Melissa walked in two minutes later. She walked up to Tricia and tapped her on the shoulder. "What's up girlfriend?" Tricia turned around. "Hey girl."

"So, have you decided where we're going?" Melissa asked.

"Yeah, we could go to the Tunnel in New York if that's cool with you." Tricia said.

"Sure. That's fine. But would you mind driving and I'll leave my car here?"

"No problem. Are you ready to go or would you like to order a drink?"

"I'm ready whenever you are," Melissa replied. They left the bar about five minutes later and headed for Tricia's black Malibu. They made small talk all the way to the club. Tricia commented Melissa on her outfit, which was a black Donna Karen strapless dress. Melissa was built like a supermodel. Although she was only five feet five inches, she had very shapely legs and a nice sized butt. She wore her hair in her usual doobie-style. It hung to the middle of her back. She also had on a diamond necklace with matching earrings and tennis bracelet. She wore a watch on her left wrist.

The line to get inside was long as usual. Tricia led Melissa to the front of the line. "Mind if we cut in?" Tricia asked in a seductive voice. The bouncer was used to hearing that kind of line from women trying to get into the club. He just kept checking the VIP list and said, "Back of the line please."

"Are you sure?" Tricia said again in the same voice. He looked up and smiled at Tricia then kissed her hand. "And how have you been Ms. Hobbs?"

"Very well and yourself." Tricia said flirtatiously.

"Why didn't you call and let me know you were coming?"

"It was a last minute decision. I hope you don't mind."

"Nah, it's cool. Is Tarik parking the car?"

"Nah. He's not here tonight. It's just me and my friend Melissa." Tricia said.

"Okay, come on in," he said as he removed the red ropes for the two ladies. A few women in the line said the word 'Bitch' a few times loud enough for Tricia and Melissa to hear. Tricia looked back and smiled on her way inside the club. Once inside, Melissa recognized one of her favorite club songs playing. "I'm going to the dance floor. This is my song girl. I'll be right back." Melissa said as she bounced towards the dance area. Tricia stood by the bar and scanned the crowd while she waited for Melissa. She noticed three men trying to dance with Melissa. Melissa turned them down instantly. Tricia even saw her flash her wedding band in a face or two. Melissa looked as if she was really enjoying herself. After two club songs, she finally returned to where Tricia stood. "I'm sorry girl. I don't get the chance to go clubbing like I used to. I don't know when the last time I've been out," she said out of breath. "Oh that's okay girl, that's why we're here. Enjoy yourself. You wanna order a drink?"

"Sure."

They went to the bar and Melissa got the attention of one of the bartenders. She ordered both drinks and paid for them. She gave Tricia hers and they found a table in the back of the club. In the next two hours Tricia discovered that Melissa was a working wife. She didn't have many friends and she'd do anything for her husband. She also learned that Melissa wanted to have a baby and that her husband finally agreed to it tonight. Melissa told her all about her relationship with Tarik and how they became friends. She tried her best to assure Tricia that their friendship has been purely platonic since the day they met. Melissa also stressed how much she loved her husband and would never cheat on him. Tricia wanted to trust Melissa. She instantly clicked with her. She even asked her if she wanted to come to the next wedding plan meeting. "Are you sure?" Melissa asked. "Yes. I just feel like I've known you forever. I really wish that I'd been more understanding and met you years ago. "It's okay Tricia. I'm feeling you too. I can see why Tarik is head over heels in love with you." She smiled sincerely. "And I would love to assist in any way that I can with the wedding."

It was Tricia's turn to get on the dance floor. She was really feeling that song 'When Can Our Love Begin'. She jumped up and Melissa followed suit. They danced for the next hour nonstop. When the DJ started playing the rap music the ladies decided that they were ready to leave. On the way out, two men approached them and asked if they would mind having a drink with them. The ladies turned the men down as gently as possible then headed out the door. Melissa was kind of happy to know that she could still get the attention of men. Tricia drove Melissa back to the bar to get her car. "Would you like to go to the diner to get something to eat?" Tricia asked.

"I can't tonight. I'm ready to go home and start a family." Melissa had a wicked grin on her face.

"Okay girl. You be safe. We meet at my mom's house for the wedding plans, so I'll call you sometime this week with directions."

"No problem. I had a good time tonight. We've got to do this again soon." Melissa said as she headed for her car.

"Yes we do. Just let me know when." Tricia responded. Tricia watched Melissa get into her silver Lexus and then she drove past her and blew the horn. Melissa blew her horn and sped off right behind Tricia.

Chapter 15

Kareem couldn't figure Simone out this time. When she usually got pissed off with him, she'd calm down in a couple of weeks. It had been a month since the last time he fucked up with her. She still refused to give in. She would hardly say two words to him when he got in from work. He'd try to make conversation with her but she would just give him short answers. But tonight would be different. He was going to have a talk with Simone and get to the bottom of the situation. He needed her to be on good terms with him. He hated it when she was upset with him. He also wanted to get with Shelly this weekend and he knew he needed to be in good standings with Simone before that happened.

He had the apartment set up in a romantic mode. He placed scented candles all around the place. He even went all out and cooked her favorite meal- Chicken Parmigiana. He placed red and yellow roses all over the bedroom floor and on the bed. Since Kareem was the only man Simone ever had sex with, he had her sprung. He knew sex would always work on Simone. He just had to make sure that she wasn't ready to kick his lying ass to the curb. He didn't know if he could handle seeing Simone with another man. If Kareem ever decided that he wanted to get married, Simone would be the one.

Simone entered the apartment with several bags of groceries. Kareem met her at the door and grabbed the bags from her hands and placed them in the kitchen. She walked to the living room and sat on the sofa. Kareem rushed to sit down next to her. He took off her shoes and began rubbing her feet. She held her head back and moaned. Kareem could always make her body respond to his touches no matter what her mouth said. "Are you hungry baby? I made your favorite." He went into the kitchen to make their plates before she could respond. Kareem returned and put their food on the dining room table. He went to the bedroom and grabbed her slippers. He slipped them on her feet and led her to the table. He pulled her chair and placed the dinner napkin in her lap. He sat opposite her and blessed the food. The aroma from the cinnamon candles was strong. They ate their meal in silence. Kareem finished first and went to the bathroom to run a hot bath. He put roses in the water along with the cinnamon scented bubble bath. He led Simone into the bathroom. He stood her in the middle of the floor and removed her clothing. Simone just stood there and allowed herself to be pampered. He didn't do this often but when he did, Simone knew she was in for one hell of a night. Kareem removed his clothes and led her to the bath. She sat between his legs and leaned back on his chest.

"Baby it's killing me that you're upset with me. I know the whole thing is my fault and I'm sorry. I want things the way they were between us."

"Kareem, did you ever stop to think that maybe I want things to change between us? I don't want to go back to the way they were. I'm tired of you disrespecting me and insulting my intelligence." She said as calmly as she could.

"What do you mean disrespecting you? I got mad respect for you."

"Oh, so you call coming to my bed in the middle of the

night respect? Stop insulting my intelligence by telling me that you're hanging out with friends from work," she said in the same calm demeanor. Kareem had never seen Simone this calm when she was pissed with him. He didn't know how to read her. This wouldn't be as easy as he thought. "Simone why won't you trust me?" He asked. Simone took her time to answer. She really didn't want to go back to the cheating thing she always threw in his face. "It's not that I don't want to trust you Kareem. You just make it impossible for me by doing stupid shit. What would you think if I came home in the middle of the night at least three times a week and told you that I was chillin' wit my girls?" She had a point Kareem thought. So he decided to go about this another way. "Simone, if I wanted to be with other women why would I put up with the constant bitching from you?" She didn't know how to respond to that. Kareem did have a point. But she was tired of him running game on her. She knew that right about now he'd say whatever he thought she wanted to hear. She decided to stand her ground.

"Kareem we have so much history together."

"Exactly." He thought that she was giving in.

"But when I really think about it, history is all we have. If we broke up today, I can't think of anything that I'd be missing," she said as she played with a few of the roses in the water.

"Baby you can't think like that. You need to try to focus on the love we have for each other." Kareem knew that sounded weak but he took a shot. He began to wash her back with the sponge as an attempt to loosen her up.

"Kareem, I feel so alone. If I'm going to feel this way, why not just be that way?" She asked as she kept her head down while he scrubbed her back.

"Simone, don't start tripping. You need to stop listening to your friends-Tricia in particular-and try to work this out with me," he said trying not to sound irritated. He moved around in front of Simone and began washing her feet and toes. She looked up at him and whispered *I love you.* "I love you too baby and I promise to make it better between us. You just have to try not to be so insecure. There's no one else for me." He kissed her passionately on the lips. She couldn't understand herself at times. She had every intention of kicking Kareem's cheating ass to the curb when she walked through the door tonight. She gave a lot of thought to what Moms said and she realized that she deserved better. She just didn't know how to let go of Kareem.

"I'll give you one more chance to get your shit together. I do mean one more chance. If I even suspect that you are cheating, yo ass is outta here." She said not believing one single word she spat out. Kareem stood her up inside the tub. She washed his body and he washed hers. Kareem led her to the bedroom and carried her over to the bed. Simone was surprised to see that Kareem went that extra mile for her with all those roses. He laid her on the bed and began licking her toes. He took in one toe at a time until he sucked each one until Simone was almost at her climax. He then straddled her and began kissing her neck. He moved down to her nipples, which were rock hard. He sucked them as if he were a baby being breastfed. She squirmed, moaned and begged for him to put his six- inch dick inside of her. But he wasn't ready yet. He wanted her to beg a little more. He needed her to understand what she would be missing if they broke up. He finally went down to the area under her belly button. He teased her thighs with his tongue for at least two minutes. She was pulling his head back up but he took his time. He put his middle finger inside her pussy and finger-fucked her. She was pumping back. He put two fingers in and found her spot. Just when she screamed *"I can't take it anymore"* he put his face on her clit and began sucking. She placed her hands on top of his head and found a rhythm. She arched her back and let out a long moan. Kareem turned over and placed her on top of him. She turned so that her back was to him. She squatted over his six inches and slid up and down until he called her name over and over. She rolled over and lay on his chest. Sleep carried her away before her eyes closed.

Chapter 16

Phil had been back from Atlanta for three weeks. Melissa wondered why he hadn't made love to her. He even rejected her advances to make love. Tonight would be different. She intended to make love to her husband. He told her that they can start a family and she would see to it that they would start tonight. While Melissa cleared the dinner dishes Phil went into the living room to watch TV. Melissa went upstairs for a quick shower. She entered the living room wearing a red g-string and bra and matching pumps. She went and stood directly in front of their fifty-two inch TV. Phil felt his dick rise the moment he noticed her. He knew he couldn't reject her tonight. Even if he wanted to, his dick told another story. Melissa turned off the TV and clicked on the radio. She had programmed two CD's. She went old school and preset tracks two, four, eleven, and twelve from R. Kelly's Twelve- Play CD. She also had in the best of Luther's double CD. From disk one she preset tracks four and ten. Disk two played tracks three and eight. She went to the sofa where he was sitting and began dancing to R. Kelly's Bump n' Grind. She made her body twist and grind like never before. She kicked her legs way over her head exposing a freshly shaven pussy. She even sat on Phil's lap and gave him a lap dance. Before the first CD was done Phil had pinned her down on the floor and made slow passionate love to his wife. Melissa enjoyed the slow lovemaking but she wanted to be fucked. Why else would she have on red? She let her husband take round one but the next round was hers. She led Phil back to the sofa and put a pillow on the floor. She got down on her knees and roughly sucked his dick. She sucked with ruthless aggression. Phil moaned and grabbed her hair. He moved her head up and down with the flow. He moved from one end of the sofa to the other. Just before he was about to cum, Melissa bent over in front of her husband and told him to fuck her doggystye. As Phil entered his wife from behind, she instantly guided him in and out of her as fast as she could. She yelled harder a few times before she lay on her stomach. Phil smacked her ass and pulled her back up. She got on all fours and looked back at him with a devilish grin on her face. He sat on his knees and made her sit on his dick. Melissa rode his dick for another five minutes before she felt the explosion of their lovemaking come to an end. They fell asleep right on the living room floor.

Tricia walked in the house to find Tarik watching TV. She was glad that he was up. She was a little horny and needed to unwind. "Hey Boo," Tricia said as she set her purse on the nightstand.

"Hey yourself." He responded.

"What are you doing up? I thought you would be sound asleep by now." Tricia said while undressing.

"I just have some things on my mind."

"Anything you wanna to talk about?" She asked as she sat beside him on the bed.

"I was just thinking about something that Melissa told me." He swung his feet to the side of the bed.

"And what's that?" Tricia asked. She sat on the bed and folded one leg under the other to get comfortable.

"When I talked to her she mentioned that she and Phil are going to start a family." Tarik said with confusion on his face.

"Yeah, I know. She said something about that earlier too. She told me that she always wanted children. I wish her luck. Shit. Better her than me!" Tricia responded. Tarik gave her a *'we'll discuss that later'* look. Now Tricia looked confused. "Aren't you happy for her? It seems like she's going to finally get what she wants." Tricia smiled.

"Boo, there's something about Phil that I don't like. Melissa is so head over heels in love with him that she won't listen to anything I say." Tarik said.

"Why don't you like Phil?"

"Well this is something that Melissa would never tell anyone else. Don't ever mention to her that I told you. And don't tell anyone else her business either!" Tarik warned.

"Come on Boo. You know you can trust me." Tricia said with a slight attitude. "So what's the deal?"

"Phil beat her up the night before they were married. She called me crying all hysterical telling me to come over to the house." Tricia was shocked as hell.

"What! Are you serious?" She put her hand to her chest. "I would have never thought anything like that by the way she talked about him all night."

"Well like I said, she's too in love to believe that he would ever hit her again. But I think that he still hits her. She denies it. So what can I do?" Tarik said hopeless.

"He beat her up and she still married him? Damn, I guess what they say is true. Once you're blinded by love, you'll put up with anything, huh?"

"Well Boo, that's why I need you," he said with an unsure look on his face. "Melissa doesn't have any female friends that she hangs out with. Phil doesn't approve of her having friends. Every time she gets close to someone, Phil makes sure that Melissa doesn't have any time to spend with the person. He has her planning parties or going out of town with him. You know things like that." Tarik explained.

"Damn. That's deep. I would have thought she has the perfect marriage by the way she speaks of Phil." Tricia said.

"And she think she has the perfect marriage. I keep trying to get her to talk about it but she refuses to discuss it wit' me. Tricia, I'm not asking you to get up in her business but I would like for you to look for any signs of abuse. She says you two hit it off well so maybe you can just be there for her. And let me know if you notice something going on with her.

"Tarik, I'll do whatever I can. But is that all you had on your mind?" she asked with a smile. She got up to go take a shower. "Tarik, meet me in the bathroom in five." She said as she walked out of the bedroom. Tarik was undressed and down the hall in four minutes. He and his bride to be had a little pre-honeymoon escapade.

Chapter 17

M elissa looked out of the window when she got out of bed. It was a nice day for April. There were leaves all over her driveway and it looked a little breezy. She was so glad that it was Friday. She had to meet Tricia and her friends to discuss a few more wedding issues. Phil had already left for the clinic. She decided to take the day off work and surprise her husband. She would take him lunch and have a nooner. It had been months since they started trying to make a baby and she wasn't pregnant yet. She called Phil's secretary to make sure that he'd be free for lunch before she made the food. Phil's secretary Alicia answered the phone in her usual pleasant voice and told Melissa that Phil was free for lunch. Melissa went to the bathroom to shower. Afterwards, she went to the market to get some groceries. She was back home at nine thirty a.m. She made a tossed salad and grilled some boneless chicken breast. She also prepared green beans and dinner rolls. She put everything in a picnic basket and went down to the wine cellar to grab a bottle of white wine. Melissa went upstairs to curl her hair. She decided to change into a brown skirt set with matching riding boots. She was out the door at twelve thirty p.m. She arrived at Phil's office at exactly one fifteen p.m. She walked up and greeted Alicia. She was told that Phil had just finished with a meeting. Melissa asked Alicia to make sure she and her husband wasn't disturbed. Alicia gave her a smile that said 'I understand' and buzzed Melissa in her husband's office. Melissa opened the door and saw Phil on the telephone. She placed the basket on the table next to the door. She opened her coat and hung it on the coat hook. Phil looked up and his eyes said it all. He polity ended his phone conversation and hung up the phone. "Hey baby. It's a surprise seeing you down here and looking quite sexy. No work today?" he asked.

"Well sweetie, I decided to come on down here to surprise you with lunch and a little sumthin-sumthin else," she said with a smile.

"Is that right?" Phil asked with a grin.

"Sure is." Melissa walked over to his desk and sat right in front of him with her legs slightly open. She wanted him to see what was in store. She began to loosen his tie. He began undoing her jacket and unzipping her skirt. She stood and Phil pushed everything from his desk. He pushed Melissa down on the desk and she pulled him on top of her. She opened her legs and he fucked her just the way she wanted. It was over twenty minutes later. Phil sat in his chair sweating and panting. Melissa went into his bathroom and washed up. When she came out, she told Phil to go shower while she prepared their lunch. Phil did what he was told and fifteen minutes later he came out to find his desk back in order and a nice picnic on the carpet. He joined Melissa and they ate their lunch.

"Melissa, I'll be home a little late tonight. One of the guys is having a poker party."

"That'll be fine Phil because I'm getting together with Tricia tonight to discuss wedding plans." She was relieved that Phil had plans or else she would have had a hard time getting out of the house. She had been meeting with Tricia for months. Phil had beaten her up last weekend because she wasn't home when he got there. She had to wear extra make-up this week to cover the black eye.

"Melissa when is their wedding? I'll be so glad when it's over. You're spending way too much time with those people."

"Phil, those people happen to be my friends. And what difference does it make? You're going out anyway." She said in an aggravated tone. Phil looked at his wife like she had lost her mind. It seemed to him that Melissa had started smart-mouthing him ever since she began hanging with these so-called friends of hers. "Melissa, watch your mouth! Who do you think you're talking to? I am not one of your friends!" He said with rage in his eyes. Melissa saw their mood change within minutes. She had to keep the peace.

"Phil I'm not trying to argue with you. We just had a wonderful time, so let's not ruin the mood. We both have plans tonight so lets leave it at that," she said with a warmer tone. Phil stopped eating.

"You're right baby. We did have a wonderful time. Let's not spoil the mood," he said with a smile.

"Let's hope that this time we got pregnant. We've been trying so hard maybe this time it'll happen." Melissa said with a smile on her face.

"Maybe." Phil answered without looking at his wife.

Chapter 18

Simone got dressed to meet the girls at Moms' house. Kareem was lying on the bed with an attitude. He wanted Simone to go bowling with him. Simone told him of her plans with the girls.

"Kareem I'm not going to argue with you about why I'm not going out with you." She sat at the vanity and painted her nails.

"You always claim I don't take you nowhere and when I try to take you out you tell me that you'd rather be wit yo girls. What's up with dat?" he said as he sat up on the bed.

"Kareem, you're full of shit! You know that we meet every week to discuss this wedding. Do you really think that I would drop my plans for you? How many times have you stood me up?" she asked as she turned around to face him. "Better yet, how many times have you dropped your plans for me? You think you slick. You just wanna hang wit me cause one of ya bitches cancelled on yo ass."

"Oh here we go," said Kareem.

"Yep, here we go. I suggest you get on the phone when I leave and call one of those hoes cause I'm outta here. Don't wait up!" she said as she walked past him out of the door.

"Damn!" Kareem said. He was really trying to be faithful to Simone. Two weeks ago she walked in the apartment while he was on the phone with Shelly. She stood behind him for five minutes listening to his phone conversation. He was just about to engage in phone sex when he turned around and noticed Simone standing there with her arms folded. He abruptly hung up the phone. He looked down to the floor. It was nothing he could say. By the look on Simone's face, she had heard enough. She walked out of the apartment and returned ten hours later drunk as a skunk. To this day she hasn't mentioned the incident. Kareem again decided right then and there that he would be a changed man. This time he came too close to losing his Boo. He's been trying for two weeks to make it up to Simone. She just won't crack this time. He's apologized too many times. He thought he still had a chance because she hadn't thrown him out. Usually Simone would have told him to go and stay with his parents. It's like she has blocked it out of her mind.

Chapter 19

Mrs. Hobbs prepared all kinds of snacks for the girls. Tricia had called and said she would be a little late and asked if her mother would handle the food. Mrs. Hobbs didn't mind. She enjoyed having the women in the house. That way she wouldn't feel too lonely. She let Tricia and her friends make most of the decisions regarding the wedding but she was adamant about the food. She would do all of the cooking. Ever since Tricia was a little girl, Mrs. Hobbs had dreamed of giving her daughter the best wedding. Tricia always enjoyed her mom's cooking. Mrs. Hobbs remembered when Tricia and Simone were teenagers that they begged and made her promise to cook at their double wedding. It wasn't going to be a double wedding but she would get the chance to cook at Tricia's. There was no telling when Kareem would get around to marrying Simone. As Mrs. Hobbs went into the dining room, the doorbell rang. It was three of the women that Tricia went to college with. They greeted Mrs. Hobbs with kisses and offered to help with the food. Mrs. Hobbs declined their offer and excused herself to the kitchen.

Simone entered the house with her key. She greeted everyone. She went to the kitchen to greet Moms and to grab something for the women to drink.

"Hey Moms," Simone said as she gave Mrs. Hobbs a gentle hug. "Where's Tricia?"

"She called and said that she'd be a little late. She should be here in a bit." Mrs. Hobbs responded. "I came in here to get the girls something to drink." Do we have the usual?" she asked as she opened the refrigerator.

"Yep. Tricia brought it by last night." Mrs. Hobbs said as she pulled out a big bowl for ice. "Go ahead and set up the drinks. I'll bring the ice in a minute," she suggested.

"Do you need any help with anything moms?"

"Naw chile. I can handle this. I've been cooking way before y'all was born," she said with a laugh. Simone did as she was told. Mrs. Hobbs entered the room with the bowl of ice. "Now you ladies have been coming here for months. If you want something get it yo self. Me and Simone will not cater to y'all tonight." She placed the bowl on the table. She then went back to the kitchen. The doorbell rang. Simone went to answer the door and saw Melissa standing on the porch. She opened the door and invited her inside. Melissa entered the house and gave Simone a warm hug. They have also become friends over the past few months. Melissa greeted the rest of the women and took a seat. Simone went in the hallway and made a brief phone call. She came back to the living room and told the ladies that Tricia would be there in ten minutes. Simone pulled out her wedding fee book. "I may as well collect the money while we wait for Tricia." Tricia asked all of her brides maids to pay for their dresses and shoes on a monthly basis. She decided it would be better on the women if they didn't have to pay in one lump sum. She also decided that there would only be three bridesmaids and her maid of honor, Simone. She wanted a nice sized wedding but not too large. Simone went around the room and collected the money and entered the correct data into the book. She put all of the money in the wedding box. Tricia put her in charge of handling all of the money that was received for the wedding. Simone was an accountant and her best friend so there was no one else she would have chosen.

Tricia entered the house moments later. She greeted the women and apologized for being late. Her mother came out of the kitchen with a tray of cheese and crackers and pickles to go with the wine and beer that the women were drinking. Tricia made herself a drink. "Okay ladies, I spoke to the stylist and he wants us all to come to the shop next month for a final fitting. You know, just to make sure everyone is the same size they were four months ago," Tricia said as she retrieved a list from her purse. "Let me find out somebody have to get their dress taken out," she said with a laugh.

"Can everyone make it on the tenth of May?" Tricia asked. Everyone checked their planners and agreed that they'll be available. "And I wanted to get your opinions on the hairstyles. I was thinking that we could wear our hair up off our faces," Tricia said.

"Tricia, you are too kind to act like our opinions matter," Chelsea joked.

"I know that's right," Andrea said with a laugh. All of the women doubled over in laughter.

"I keep trying to tell her that this is her day and we are here to assist her in any way possible," Simone said. The laughter calmed down and Tricia spoke again.

"I really would like to know what you all think. I know it's my wedding but you will be in the video too. And I don't want anyone saying that I made them look stupid or ugly, so lets hear it." The women laughed a little more but they all agreed to have their hair in an up do.

Mrs. Hobbs entered the room with a plate of hot wings and a tossed salad. Tricia got up to get the paper plates. Melissa joined her in the kitchen and grabbed the napkins and plastic ware. The women continued to drink and eat until well past midnight. They discussed a few more things about the wedding and then turned their meeting into a bitch session. Melissa looked at her watch several times during the past hour. She was having a good time with the girls and was not ready to call it a night. She excused herself and went into the hallway and pulled out her cell phone. She dialed home to see if Phil had made it in. There was no answer so she hung up and called his cell phone. She got the voicemail and left a message saying that she would be out later than expected. Melissa calmed down a little after she made her phone call. She would be able to stay a while longer cause Phil was still out. She just hoped that she made it home before he did.

"Melissa, is everything ok?" Tricia asked. She noticed that Melissa had a concerned look on her face.

"Oh yeah. I was just calling to check on Phil. He went out with some friends and he's not home yet," she smiled.

"Do you have to go? Cause I was just getting ready to ask the girls if they wanted to chill out here a while longer."

"That sounds good to me," Melissa said.

Chapter 20

Mrs. Hobbs left the women downstairs and she went to bed. They continued to drink and talk for the next several hours. It was almost daybreak when the women started to leave. Melissa was almost drunk. She was scared as hell to go home. But she knew she had to go and face her husband. She said goodbye to Tricia and Simone.

"Are you going to be able to drive, girl?" Simone asked.

"Yep, I'll be fine. I'll call you when I get in to let you know I arrived safely." She kissed their cheeks and left.

Tricia and Simone stayed up and talked some more. "Simone, how are things with you and Kareem? Is he still cutting up?"

"Girl, please! You know Kareem is gonna always be Kareem. He's going to cut up for as long as he's alive." Simone responded with slurred speech.

"Simone? Now I'm not trying to start anything but if you know that he's a fuck-up then why are you still putting up with his shit?"

"Well believe it or not, Mr. Kareem's days are numbered. I am gonna let his ass go."

"Yeah, yeah, yeah. You said all dis shit before," Tricia said. She was as drunk as Simone. She was tired of hearing Simone say the same thing.

"Look, lets not talk about Kareem ok?" Simone said. "I'd

like to know if you are nervous or not? You are going to be married in less than three months."

"Yeah, I know. Simone I'm too excited to be nervous. I just can't wait to be married to Tarik. Dat's my baby! I love him so much." She lay across the sofa on her back. Simone made another drink for Tricia.

"You know, I am so happy for you Trish. I wish you all the happiness in the world. Tarik is so lucky to have you in his life." Tricia got up to sip the drink. She reached over to give Simone a hug and fell to the floor. Simone grabbed her arm and helped her back to the sofa. Tricia laughed. "Damn, I must have had one too many."

"Tricia, do you think I'm sexy?"

"Girl please! How many times have I said I wish I had yo body?" You know you sexy so whatchu talkin 'bout?"

"Well I just don't understand why Kareem don't want me." She began to cry. Tricia sat up on the sofa with Simone sitting on the floor between her legs. She laid Simone's head on her lap. She pulled her hair back out of her face. "Simone it's not you, it's him. He's just not ready for the things that you want. You have so much to offer any man and if Kareem can't see that then he's the one missing out." Tricia slid on the floor next to her sister friend. She hugged her tight and rubbed her back. She reached over and grabbed her drink. Her head began to spin. "Simone I think we should call it a night. You're staying right?" Simone wiped her eyes and shook her head yes.

"Tricia, I'm sorry for getting all emotional."

"Shut up Simone! We know how you do when you drink." They both laughed. They sat in silence for a few minutes. Simone put her hand on Tricia's leg and began to rub gently up and down. Tricia laid her head on the sofa. Simone began to explore Tricia's body with her hands. She rubbed her arms and massaged her breasts. She was a little nervous at first but when Tricia didn't object she continued. Simone slid her hand under Tricia's blouse and played with her nipples. Tricia moaned and moved her body down to get more comfortable. Simone pulled Tricia's shirt over her head. She laid Tricia on the floor and began sucking her nipples. Tricia put her hands on Simone's head and guided her to go faster and harder. Simone pulled Tricia's pants down and slid her thong down below her knees. Tricia just lay there and played with her pussy. She began to finger-fuck herself. While Simone sat back and watched, she played with her own erect nipples until she felt herself getting wet. She put her face in between Tricia's thighs and let her tongue explore her body. She started to gently suck between Tricia's legs. Tricia was enjoying every minute. She grabbed the back of Simone's head and forced her to suck harder. She was moaning so loud that Simone had to cover her mouth with her hands. As soon as Simone put her hands over Tricia's mouth, Tricia began to suck her fingers. She took each finger into her mouth nice and slow. She sucked them like she was sucking a lollipop. Simone began sucking even harder. She was a little aggressive but Tricia loved it. Tricia wrapped her legs around Simone's neck and yelled,

"Damn Tarik, you eating the hell outta this pussy Boo!" Simone came to a complete stop. She removed Tricia's legs and sat up on her knees.

"Bitch, I know you didn't just call me Tarik! I know he's never fucked you like this." Tricia opened her eyes and saw Simone sitting on her knees. She slowly pulled up her pants and screamed, "What the fuck are you doing, Simone?" Simone stood up to pull her shirt back down. "Don't you mean what the fuck are *we* doing?" She said in a sarcastic tone. Tricia now felt sober. She leaped over to Simone and put her hands around her neck. "Bitch, ima fuck you up!" Simone backed away from Tricia's grip and held her hands in front of her for protection. "Wait Tricia. I'm sorry."

"You're sorry?" Tricia grabbed Simone by her hair and

flung her into the coffee table. Simone stood up. Tricia ran over and knocked her back down on the floor. She balled up her fist and punched Simone in her left eye. Simone pushed Tricia off of her and ran towards the door. Tricia was too fast. She met Simone at the door and put her hands around her neck. Simone was crying and trying to pry Tricia's hands from her neck. Tricia spun Simone around and made the lamp fall.

All the commotion brought Mrs. Hobbs downstairs. She saw Tricia choking Simone and tried to get her hands from around her neck. Tricia did not let go of Simone's neck. Mrs. Hobbs had to squeeze herself in the middle of the girls. "Tricia let go of her neck! The girl can't breathe." Mrs. Hobbs pleaded. "This bitch deserves to die momma!" Simone's body was getting weak. She couldn't fight Tricia any longer. Mrs. Hobbs finally pulled Tricia's hands from Simone's neck. "What the hell is going on here?" she asked. Simone was in a corner crying and rubbing her neck. Tricia was trying to get at Simone again but Mrs. Hobbs blocked her way. "Tricia, just calm down a minute. What happened?" Tricia was breathing hard and she had tears in her eyes. "Simone get the fuck outta here before I kill yo ass this time!" Mrs. Hobbs made Tricia sit on the sofa. "Simone, are you okay? Would one of you tell me what happened please?" Tricia tried to stand up but her mother got right in her space making her sit back down. Simone touched her nose and felt the blood oozing out. She grabbed the chair for support and pulled herself up.

"Tricia I never planned for this to happen. I really am sorry," Simone cried.

"You got that right you sorry ass bitch. No wonder Kareem don't want yo ass!"

"Alright ladies stop it before you all say something that you'll regret. Simone maybe you should leave now and let Tricia calm down some."

"Moms all I want is for Tricia to hear me out."

"Simone if you don't get yo black ass outta here!" Tricia said as she attempted to get up again. Mrs. Hobbs pushed her down and told Simone to leave.

"I think it'll be best if I talked to Tricia alone Simone. I'll call to check on you later." Simone gathered her things and went to the door. She looked back and mumbled, "Tricia I'm sorry." Then she left.

Chapter 21

S imone sat in her car for twenty minutes before she drove home. She was troubled about the incident that just took place. Simone never planned for any of this to happen. She didn't even know that she had those kinds of feelings inside of her. The last thing she wanted was to jeopardize her friendship with Tricia. She held a tight grip to the steering wheel. She never saw Tricia so upset. She didn't know if their friendship was repairable or not. Tears were strolling down her face causing her vision to blur. She pulled her car over and put her head on the wheel. She hit the horn and yelled, *"oh my goodness what did I do?"* She closed her eyes and let the tears fall.

• • •

Melissa entered her house at four thirty in the morning. She didn't know if Phil was home or not. She went over her limit with the drinking tonight. She tried to be as quiet as possible when going up the steps. She began to undress on the staircase. She was going to skip the shower tonight and get right into bed. She opened the bedroom door and saw Phil sitting on the edge of the bed. She stood up tall and tried to hide the fact that she was drunk. Phil looked up and saw his wife stagger towards the bed. He leaped over to Melissa and punched her in the chest. Melissa hit the floor immediately. *"What the fuck were you doing out until this time in the morning?"* Whoop...whack...smack. Melissa felt her stomach turn.

She tried to crawl to the bathroom but Phil kicked her in the stomach and she vomited right on the floor. *"You fuckin' drunk bitch! I told you to stop hangin' 'round those ghetto ass people."* Melissa felt a little sober. She tried to cover her face from the punches that Phil was throwing. "Phil please…stop! You're h…hurting me!" Phil grabbed Melissa to her feet and threw her against the wall. Her head hit the wall and she slid to the floor. Phil kicked Melissa in the chest and legs. She balled herself up in a corner and cried out. Melissa didn't know how much longer Phil beat her but it seemed like a lifetime. She lay on the floor in a puddle of blood. Phil looked down at her. *"Why do you make me do these things to you Melissa? Don't you know how much I love you?"* He closed the bedroom door as he left.

Chapter 22

Tricia sat on her mother's sofa and cried for the next two hours. Mrs. Hobbs sat next to her daughter and tried to get her to talk. Tricia didn't want to tell her mother what happened so she just kept telling her that Simone had crossed the line.

"What do you mean crossed the line Tricia? You and Simone have been friends for as long as I can remember and I've never seen you two so upset with each other. Now I understand that you don't want to talk about it right know, but I'm here whenever you're ready." She placed Tricia's head in her lap. "Go on and let it all out chile."

"Momma would you call Tarik and ask him to come pick me up please?" she asked between sniffles. "Anything you want baby, but you sure you don't wanna stay here?"

"No momma. I just wanna go home!" Mrs. Hobbs went into the kitchen and made the call. She re-entered the living room and sat back down beside Tricia. Tricia looked around the room. "Mama, I'll come over tomorrow and clean up this mess. I'm sorry for everything."

"Baby don't worry 'bout dis here mess. I'll fix it." She hugged her daughter tightly.

"Thanks mama."

Tarik parked the car in the driveway and rang the doorbell. Mrs. Hobbs opened the door and gestured for him to come in. Tarik gave her a hug and kissed her cheek. He looked around the room and turned to Mrs. Hobbs. "What happened in here?"

"Oh the ladies got a little carried away tonight that's all." Mrs. Hobbs smiled.

"Is everything ok? You sounded a little upset on the phone," he said as he took a seat on the sofa. Just as Mrs. Hobbs was about to answer, Tricia came down stairs. "Yep, everything is fine. Me and the girls had a tad bit too much fun." She smiled. Mrs. Hobbs stared at her daughter. Tricia had gone upstairs to clean herself up. She looked as if nothing was wrong. Tricia went over to hug and kiss Tarik.

"Are you ready?" She asked.

"Whenever you are," he said. Mrs. Hobbs was still standing there dumbfounded. Tricia turned to Tarik and asked him to wait in the car. "I'll be right out. Just let me grab my things." Tarik said goodbye to Mrs. Hobbs and went to start the car. Tricia turned to her mother and said that she would tell Tarik tomorrow. And right now all she wanted was to get some sleep. Mrs. Hobbs said she understood and walked Tricia to the door. She told them to be safe and then she started cleaning her house. She just wondered what the fight was all about.

• • •

Tricia took off her clothes and lay across the bed.

"What's wrong Tricia? And don't tell me nothing cause I know you better than that." Tricia turned her body around to face Tarik.

"I'm just tired that's all." She gave a weak smile.

"Tricia, what happened?" She looked at Tarik and knew he wouldn't let up until she told him something.

"Simone and I had a fight tonight." She said and began sobbing again.

"What happened Boo?" He asked as he took off his clothes. Tricia put her head in the pillow and cried harder. Tarik went by her side and tried to comfort her.

"Trish why are you crying? You two are always fighting. It'll be ok." Tricia sat up in the bed.

"No baby we had a fist fight."

"What?" Tarik stared at her in disbelief. "What do you mean fist fight? Tricia, what happened?" He asked as he sat down next to her on the bed.

"I mean that Simone and I have finally reached the point of no return." Tarik didn't know what to think.

"Tricia, how much did you have to drink?"

"We were all drinking Tarik and I'll admit that I was a little wasted but right about now, I am well and sober."

Tarik didn't know what to say. He knew Tricia didn't want to talk about whatever happened so he decided to let it go for the night. He just sat back and held her in his arms.

"Tricia, did you get a chance to talk to Melissa tonight?"

"No, not really but she seemed nervous most of the night. She left late and was supposed to call me to let me know that she arrived home safely. Now that I think about it, she didn't call me at all. Boo, she was drunk when she left. You call her to make sure that she's okay." Tarik pulled off his boxers.

"Okay Boo I'll call her first thing in the morning."

"Tarik call her now please. I would feel terrible if something happened and we waited 'til tomorrow to check up on her." Tarik was tired. He sighed long and hard before he got up to call Melissa. He dialed the number and the phone rang five times before the voicemail came on. He left a message for her to call him and Tricia as soon as she got the message. He climbed back into bed and pulled Tricia closer to him. He was asleep in no time.

Chapter 23

S imone stayed in bed all day Saturday. She just lay there with her eyes open. She didn't get any sleep when she came home this morning. Kareem was not home when she walked through the door. Simone was so wrapped up in her own drama that for a change she didn't care that he wasn't home nor did she care where he was. She just hoped that he would stay gone for a few more hours because she needed this time to herself. She kept replaying the events in her mind. Simone started to cry again. *What the fuck was I thinking?* She wondered. Tricia was the only true friend that she had. Now she had to think of a way to fix their relationship.

She sat up on the bed. She put her hand on the receiver to call Mrs. Hobbs' house. Just as she was about to dial the number, she heard Kareem put the key in the door. She jumped back and put the phone back in its cradle. Kareem walked into the apartment and headed straight to the bedroom. Simone sat on the side of the bed not saying a word. He walked into the bedroom and expected Simone to go off on him. He looked at the back of her head and tried to think of a lie. He didn't expect her to be at home since she and Tricia usually went to the gym on Saturdays. "Hey baby." Kareem said. "I've been trying to call you all night to let you know that I would be over at my parents' house." He sat on the bed next to her. She turned to him with blood-red eyes and just cried. Kareem tried to get Simone to tell him what was bothering her. She kept telling him that she didn't want to talk about it. She let her man hold her for the rest of the morning.

• • •

When she awoke, Melissa tried to get up from of the floor. Her legs were numb. Her head was pounding and she smelled terrible. She tried to call out for Phil but her jaw was too sore. Melissa turned towards the nightstand and saw that the clock read 1:28 p.m. She needed help and didn't know what to do. She knew she had to get to the phone. She tried to crawl to the nightstand but her legs were no use to her. She finally used one arm to pull her body across the room. Melissa was able to get close enough to pull the phone cord and knock it on the floor. She dialed the number and hoped that someone would answer.

A voice answered. "Hello?"

"P...please c...c...come and help m...m...me. I'm hurt. Co...come alone. Don't tell him anything right now. I...I can't m...move." That was the only thing she was able to utter before she passed out.

"Oh my goodness! Melissa? Melissa?" She heard the dial tone. Tricia ran around the apartment gathering her things. She found a hat and threw it on her head. She had an appointment to get her hair done in an hour. She grabbed her keys and headed out the door. In the car, she dialed Melissa again but kept getting the voicemail. Tricia drove 60mph in a 40mph zone. She could care less about the police. The only thing on her mind was getting to Melissa. She pulled into Melissa's driveway twenty minutes later. This was her first trip to Melissa's house. It was huge. She went to the door and twisted the knob. It was locked. *Shit! How in the hell am I supposed to get in?* She thought. She followed a pavement path that led her to the backyard. She saw a door and again turned the knob. It too was locked. Melissa took her hat from her head and wrapped it around her hand. She hoped like hell that there wasn't an alarm. She pushed her fist through one of the glassed sections of the door and broke a window. To her surprise there was no alarm. She reached inside and unlocked the door. Tricia was now in Melissa's kitchen. She was in awe. Melissa had one of the most beautiful kitchens that she'd ever saw. She walked through the kitchen and found the dining room. She felt like she was in a mansion. Tricia began to wonder where Melissa could be inside the house. She roamed throughout the house and searched for Melissa. Tricia believed that she covered the entire first level. She found the staircase and went to the second level. As soon as she reached the top, she saw a door to her left. She opened the door and whispered Melissa's name. It was a bedroom but Melissa was not there. Tricia proceeded down the hall and opened another door and found a bathroom. Finally, she opened the second door to her right. She cautiously entered the room. She spotted Melissa lying on the floor in a corner.

"Oh my goodness! Melissa? Melissa?" Tricia kneeled down beside her and checked for a pulse. Melissa barely had one. Tricia spotted the phone on the floor next to Melissa. She was about to dial 911 when she felt Melissa touch her arm. Tricia dropped the phone and grabbed Melissa's hand. "Melissa, what happened to you? Can you talk or move?" Melissa told Tricia that she could talk a little but was unable to move her legs.

"Melissa, I don't know what to do. You need to get to a hospital. I'm going to call for an ambulance."

"Tricia, p...please don't c...c...call anyone. I do not want anyone else to s..see me like this." Melissa wrinkled her face from the pain of talking.

"What are you talking about? You can't move and you can barely talk. Lissa you need professional help. At least let me call Tarik."

Melissa shook her head no several times. She tightened

the grip on Tricia's arm and pulled her closer to her mouth. She whispered in Tricia's ear.

"Look, I'm a nurse. I'll just tell you what to do, okay?" she said very slowly.

"Melissa, where's your husband?" Melissa turned her head away from Tricia at the mentioning of her husband. Melissa tried to shrug her shoulders but the pain prevented it.

Tricia put her purse in a chair and took off her heels. "Melissa, I don't know if I can do this without hurting you. I'm scared to move you."

"Just grab my upper body and slide me up on the bed. It's my legs that are in pain. I won't be able to help you so be prepared to carry all of my weight." Tricia bent down and prepared to grab Melissa's upper body. "Tricia if I...I scream in p...p...pain, ignore it and k...keep going."

"Lissa, are you sure?"

"Yep, I've been on this floor seems like all night." Melissa's speech was getting better since she was talking. Her mouth was dry so she asked Tricia to get her a glass of water.

Chapter 24

Tricia cleaned Melissa as best as she could. She even gave her a bed bath. Even though it was her first time, Tricia did a pretty good job of cleaning Melissa. She tried to convince Melissa that she needed to be in a hospital. Melissa finally broke down and told Tricia to call one of the doctors she knew and trusted from the hospital where she worked. Tricia called the number and said exactly what she and Melissa rehearsed. Dr. Michael Carter would be there in a little over an hour.

Tricia sat on the bed next to Melissa and held her hand. "Lissa, you know that you can talk to me about anything." Melissa began to cry for the first time since she'd awakened this afternoon. "Melissa, did Phil do this to you?"

Melissa looked up through swollen eyes. "Tricia why would you think that my husband would do something like this to me?" Her speech was a little slurred because her jaw was swollen. Tricia just looked at her with sorrow in her eyes.

"Melissa, I already know about your past with Phil. Tarik told me what happened on the night before you two were married. He's so worried that Phil is still hitting you." Melissa turned her head to the other side and spoke softly.

"I can't believe T...T...Tarik told you something that was so p...p...p...private."

"It really wasn't like that. Tarik loves you and he's just worried. He asked me to keep an eye out for any signs of abuse." Melissa tried to turn her body towards Tricia but winced in pain. Tricia ran to the other side of the bed.

"What are you trying to do, Lissa?"

"I want to t...turn on my side." She helped turn Melissa on her side. It was too painful so she remained on her back. Melissa patted the side of the bed and gestured for Tricia to sit. Tricia went to sit and held Melissa's hand again.

"P...promise that I will tell you everything but not until M...Michael leaves okay?" Tricia smiled and kissed Melissa on the forehead.

"Whatever you're comfortable with, Melissa. I need to call Tarik and let him know that I'm alright."

"Tricia, please don't tell Tarik about this. I know it's a lot to ask but I will tell you everything in a little while." *Ring ring.*

"That must be Michael. Let him up please." Tricia went down to open the door. She introduced herself and led Dr. Carter to the bedroom. After seeing her bruises, Dr. Carter asked if he could examine Melissa alone. Tricia went to the kitchen to make tea. She called Tarik's cell phone and left a message that she'd be home around 8pm. She came upstairs twenty minutes later with the tray of tea and knocked on the door. Dr. Carter told her it was okay for her to come inside. He asked Melissa if it was okay that he talked in front of Tricia. She said it was okay and he began explaining all of Melissa's injury's as he bandaged different parts of her body. Dr. Carter spoke softly. "Melissa, it is a miracle that you are not unconscious. You have a broken toe, your legs are swollen and bruised, you have two fractured ribs and your left arm is sprained. You have a black eye and your face is very swollen. You need to go to the hospital." Tricia just twinged as Dr. Carter recited all of Melissa's injures.

"Would anyone like some tea?" Tricia asked.

"I think I will have a cup." Dr. Carter said.

"Not for me." Melissa said between sobs.

"Melissa, what the hell happened to you?" Dr. Carter asked.

"I would really rather not talk about it right now, Mike." Michael Carter looked over at Tricia for an answer but she shrugged her shoulders and kept stirring the cup of tea.

"Melissa, you don't have to tell me what happened, but I insist on taking you to the hospital. Tricia, would you mind helping her get dressed while I make a couple of calls?"

"Sure Dr. Carter."

"Please, call me Mike," he said sincerely. "Mike, are you sure you can't take care of me here?" Melissa asked.

"I'm sorry but there's nothing more I can do for you here. May I use a phone?"

"Yeah, you can go downstairs for privacy. Mike please do not take me to St. Barnabas. I do not need co-workers all in my business."

"I'll make arrangements for you to go to Union County," he said as he closed the bedroom door behind him.

Tricia sat on the hospital bed next to Melissa. "Is there anyone you want me to call?"

"Actually there is. Please dial Phil's cell for me." Tricia looked at Melissa like she was a ghost.

"Girl, please tell me that you are joking." Tricia stood to get a closer look at Melissa's face.

"Tricia I need to let my husband know what's going on."

"I can't believe you Lissa. It's his fault that you're here in the first place."

"It's not all his fault. Please dial this number for me." Melissa called out the number while Tricia dialed and handed the hospital phone to Melissa. "Damn, the voicemail came on." She handed the phone back to Tricia. Tricia pulled a chair from the corner of the room and placed it directly in front of Melissa. "Now tell me what happened Melissa." Melissa pushed a button on the automatic bed and raised her head. She spoke very slowly.

"Well when I got in this morning, Phil was waiting up for me. He asked what I was doing coming home at such an hour. I didn't think he'd be there since I called him several times and he didn't answer the phone. Well, he was there and not too pleased to see that I was drunk. He didn't give me a chance to explain anything. He rushed at me with his fists. I fell to the floor and vomited. I tried to get to the bathroom to clean up but he kept me on the floor in that corner. I remember covering my face for protection. I don't know how much longer Phil hit me but the last thing I remember was Phil standing by the door asking me why I make him do such things to me. He closed the door and walked out of the bedroom. Tricia, I haven't seen him since." Melissa began to cry again.

"Damn Melissa, I'm not going to sit here and tell you that I know how you feel because I'd be lying. But Tarik and I are here for you. You can just come and stay with us until you're better." Tricia began to look through her purse for her cell phone.

"Tricia, you still can't tell Tarik anything about this." Tricia stopped what she was doing.

"Why not? You need our help Melissa."

"I don't know how much Tarik told you about my wedding but it was serious. Tarik has been protecting me since high school. When he found out what happened between Phil and me, he swore that if Phil ever hit me again he'd kill him. Tricia I honestly believe that Tarik will kill Phil." Tricia sat back in the chair and sighed heavily.

"Melissa, what am I supposed to tell Tarik? He's already worried about you. When I told him that you didn't call to let me know that you arrived home safely last night, he left you a message."

"Damn Tricia. We need to think of something."

"No, no, no, not we! *You* need to think of something. I

am not going to lie to him about something like this." Tricia said seriously.

"I know I have no right to ask you this. But I love my husband and I don't want to see anything happen to him. Most of what happened was my fault. I knew how Phil would react to my coming in the house that late and drunk on top of that."

Tricia looked at Melissa in disbelief. "Well Melissa, I can't tell you what to do but I do think that you should let us help you. Dr. Carter said that you would be in the hospital for at least a week. What are you going to do?" Melissa sighed.

"I'll call Tarik in a few days and let him know that I'm alright. In the meantime will you tell him that you've been talking to me and that I'm okay?" I just need time for Phil and me to work this thing out. Please don't tell anyone about this Tricia. Not even Simone." Tricia looked away from Melissa.

"You don't have to worry about that, Simone and I are not speaking right now." Melissa tried to sit up but winced in pain.

"What happened? You two had a disagreement?" Tricia turned to look Melissa in the eyes.

"No, Melissa. Simone and I had a fist fight last night after everyone left Mom's house." Tricia now had tears in her eyes as she replayed the incident in her head.

"And I really don't want to talk about it right now." Melissa grabbed Tricia's hand and gently tugged her down on the bed.

"Tricia, I understand that you do not want to talk about it. You really seem upset. Are you going to be alright?" Tricia wiped her eyes and shook her head yes.

"Well Lissa, I have to leave now. Tarik has left me two messages and I need to cook dinner. If you need anything, just call me okay?" Melissa shook her head yes. Tricia bent down to kiss her forehead and then headed out the door. Tricia turned around and looked at Melissa.

"I hate to leave you here alone like this."

"Tricia if you stay then Tarik would suspect something.

I'll be fine. I need time alone to think anyway. Go home and get some rest. Tricia thanks for everything." Melissa lowered her bed and tried to get some sleep. Tricia backed slowly out of the room.

Chapter 25

K areem walked in the bedroom to find Simone in the bed crying again. She had been crying every night for the past two weeks. He constantly tried to get her to tell him what happened but she refused every time. He sat on the bed next to her and just wrapped his arms around her body.

"Simone just call Tricia and work this thing out with her. I know that whatever happened can be fixed." Simone turned on her back and faced him.

"Kareem, weren't you on your way out?" He looked at Simone with surprise.

"What?"

She sat up on the bed Indian style.

"You heard what the hell I said. Just go and leave me alone! You don't even like Tricia, so stop acting like you really care whether we make up or not!" Kareem stood and paced the room.

"Simone, I'm just trying to help you. You can cut dat gangsta shit, aiight? I been tryna be here for yo ass all week and all you been doin' is taking yo attitudes out on me. If you wanna sit here and feel sorry for yourself, then go 'head cause I'm outta here today. I'm sicka sittin round here getting cursed out for no reason." He got up and left. Simone stared at the bedroom door for at least five minutes after Kareem left.

She got up and went to take a shower. Today she had a plan. When she finished getting dressed, she drove to Moms' house for a talk. She walked up the three steps and rang the doorbell. Mom's opened the door and welcomed Simone inside of the house. Simone sat in her favorite chair after she took off her jacket. "So how have you been baby?" Mom's asked. Simone looked at moms with tears in her eyes. "Moms I can't make this thing with Tricia go away. I tried calling her but she won't take my calls. I don't know what else to do." Mrs. Hobbs sat down. "Simone, you know that I never get in the middle of none of y'alls thangs. Tricia didn't tell me what happened and I don't want you to tell me either. You all will have to work this out on your own." Simone grabbed a tissue from the box on the coffee table and started to cry hard. Mrs. Hobbs came to comfort Simone. She rubbed her hand up and down Simone's back. "Let it out chile." After another twenty minutes when it seemed like Simone was calming down, Mrs. Hobbs sat back on the sofa.

"Simone, you are going to hafta pull yourself together. I don't know what happened but I do know that you sittn' round crying not gonna change thangs. Tricia will come around. Y'all are too close for her to forget about the friendship that you built over the years." Simone turned her head away.

"I think I really blew it this time, Moms. You think you could talk to her for me, please?" Mrs. Hobbs turned away from Simone. She didn't have the heart to tell her that Tricia didn't want to have anything to do with her. "Simone that is between you and Trish. You know that I'll always be here for you. You are the daughter I didn't have the chance to have but I'm not getting involved. I need you to respect that, okay?" Simone shook her head yes and settled down. Mrs. Hobbs offered her something to eat but Simone declined. She gathered her things and kissed Mrs. Hobbs on the cheek. She opened the door and thanked Moms for listening.

Chapter 26

"Tarik, where are you?" Tricia yelled as she stacked the shoes by the closet. The shoemaker finally finished making the shoes for the wedding. She had gone to pick them up since it was on her way from the nail salon.

"I'm in the shower, Boo," he yelled over the music from the radio. Tricia opened the bathroom door and stared at his physique. Tarik was the sexiest man she'd ever known. Those almond shaped eyes were the sexiest thing to her. He had a six-pack to die for. His arms were perfectly cut and that smile of his made her blush every time she saw it. She quickly got undressed and joined him in the shower.

"Hey you," she said as she slid her hands down his chest.

"Where were you off to early this morning?" He asked as he turned to face her.

"I went to get my nails done and to pick up the shoes for my girls. You and the guys are going to get the final fitting for the tuxedos today right?"

"Yep. We're leaving at 2:30. How are the plans coming along?"

"Everything is good. I just need to make one little adjustment with my bridal party." Tarik looked at her and shook his head side to side.

"Tricia, now what are you going to do?" She began to wash his back with the scrub brush.

"Well, you know that Simone and I haven't made up. I don't want her in our wedding." Tarik grabbed the brush from her hand.

"What do you mean you don't want her in the wedding? She's your best friend. I think it's time for you two to cut the shit and work this thing out," he said as he lathered body wash on a cloth.

"Boo, it's not that easy. We are never going to be like we were even if we do make up. Right now, I don't have anything to say to her." Tricia leaned against the wall to enjoy a breast message. "I am going to ask Melissa to be my maid of honor." Tarik stopped what he was doing.

"Tricia, this is a serious decision. Are you sure you don't want your best friend by your side?"

"Baby I have thought about this and I don't want her there. I'm going to see Melissa today. I'll just ask her then." Tarik placed the cloth on the shower hook and used his hands to explore Tricia's body. He felt her ass and squeezed it a little. He placed her under the shower to remove all of the suds from her body.

"If this is what you want then I support you on the decision."

She smiled and kissed him passionately. Tarik moved Tricia against the shower wall. He lifted her left leg and placed it around his hip. Tricia grabbed the back of his head for support. He gently slid his throbbing penis inside of her. Tricia moved her body up and down his shaft for a few minutes. She put her other leg on Tarik's other hip and began to move faster. Tarik kissed her neck and talked in her ear. Tricia loved when Tarik whispered in her ear while they were making love. "Tarik... baby... I'ma... bout... to cum."

"Mmummm hummm, cum then baby. Cum all over me," he whispered in her ear.

"Boo, I want you to cum wit me. Ohh, Tarik I'm cumming.

Ohhhhh, ohhhhhhh, ohhhh, damn Boo." She screamed in ecstasy as her body jerked viciously. Tarik put Tricia down and turned her around. He bent her over and entered her from behind. He proceeded to pump in and out of her for a few more minutes. Tricia started to pump back. She did this faster with each stroke. Tarik leaned on her body and whispered in her ear. "Baby, it's cumming! It's cumming right now!" Tricia pushed Tarik from behind her and got on her knees. She pulled his enlarged penis in her mouth and began to suck until the white cream began to splurt out. He held his head back and enjoyed the moment. "Damn Trish. I love you so much."

"And I love you too, Boo." They showered and stepped out of the bathtub with huge smiles on their faces. Tricia walked into the bedroom and began searching through drawers. She found a shirt to match the jeans she wore and put it on without ironing. Tarik had two hours to pick up his cousin, Will.

"Trish, you're going to see Melissa now?"

"Yep." Tricia said without looking at him.

"Be sure to tell her I said what's up." Tricia glanced at him from the corner of her eye. She felt very uncomfortable not telling Tarik that his friend was in trouble.

"Did you notice any signs of abuse?"

"Um, not really. Melissa and I have been together almost every night this week and I haven't noticed anything. She's been real cool when talking about Phil."

"Are you sure Tricia? I just have this gut feeling that she's in trouble." Tricia continued to get dressed without looking Tarik directly in his eyes.

"Well, I'll keep my eyes open but I really think everything's okay." Tarik went to Tricia and kissed her on the lips.

"Okay, Boo I'm out. See you later. He grabbed his things and left. "Damn." Tricia said under her breath when she heard the front door close. She put on her sneakers and left.

Chapter 27

M elissa was in the hospital room packing her things. She was able to move around much better this week. Tricia would be there to pick her up any minute. She had a bandage around her waist. Her foot was in an open toe cast. But she was able to walk with a cane. The bruises on her face were not too bad. She could use make-up to cover the marks. She sat on the bed and stared at the phone. She wondered why Phil wasn't there with her. She had been calling his office all week. She was being told that Phil was out of town and wouldn't be back until Monday. Melissa picked up the phone and dialed Phil's cell phone. There was no answer. She then called the house but kept getting the voicemail. Melissa put her head down as the tears began to fall from her eyes. Tricia knocked on the door and entered the room.

"Hey Melissa, are you ready?" Melissa didn't want Tricia to see her crying. She knew Tricia would ask why and she didn't want to explain that it was about Phil. Melissa wiped her eyes and shook her head.

"I've already packed my things. I was just waiting for you. Did you park in the lot?" Tricia grabbed the duffel bag and helped Melissa to her feet.

"I parked right out front in the handicapped zone. So we better get a move on." Melissa grabbed her cane and followed Tricia. They passed by the nurses' station and saw Dr. Carter.

Melissa stood directly in front of him and smiled. "Mike, thank you." Dr. Carter put his hands up to detest Melissa's words. "There's no need to thank me, Lissa. I know that you would do the same thing for me. I'm glad to see you're doing better. Remember, if you ever want to talk, I'm just a phone call away." He smiled and then kissed Melissa on her cheek. "Thanks again, Mike. Don't be surprised if I take you up on your offer." She kissed his cheek then followed Tricia to the elevator. "Goodbye Dr. Carter." Tricia said as she waited for Melissa to catch up to her. Dr. Carter waved bye to the ladies as he watched the elevator doors close.

Melissa gave Tricia the keys so she could open the door to her house. Tricia entered the house with caution. She wasn't sure if Phil was there or not. Melissa limped in behind her and took a seat on the sofa. Tricia sat on the loveseat opposite her.

"Melissa, how do you feel?" Melissa sighed and pushed a strand of hair from her face.

"Tricia, I know you're not going to understand but I miss Phil. I need to know where he is and if he's alright." Tricia sat in silence because she didn't want to get too involved in Melissa's business. "Phil hasn't called my cell phone once. Apparently, he hasn't been here either cause I've been calling to check every day." Melissa saw how uncomfortable Tricia looked and decided to change the subject. "Tricia, are you hungry? Let's go in the kitchen and find us something to eat." Tricia stood.

"I guess I am a little hungry. Besides, I have something to ask you." Tricia helped Melissa to her feet and they proceeded to the kitchen.

"What are you in the mood for, Tricia?"

"Anything as long as it's non-fat. I can't afford to put on any extra weight so close to the wedding. I just had my final fitting on Monday. What are you doing trying to walk around on that foot? Just tell me where everything is and I'll make us a nice chicken salad."

"It's okay Tricia, it's only a broken toe. I need to get used to walking on it anyhow."

"Melissa, don't argue with me on this one. Have a seat please." Melissa looked at Tricia and smiled.

"Okay, you win. I'm a little tired anyway." Melissa pointed out all the ingredients for the salad and Tricia began to prepare their lunch. It was quiet for a minute while Tricia washed off the lettuce.

"Melissa, have you called your parents to let them know what happened?" Melissa turned her head away from Tricia when she spoke.

"Tricia, my parents and I haven't spoken in four years. They were not pleased when Phil and I announced our engagement. They told me that if I married Phil, they weren't going to have anything to do with me. I was so in love with Phil that I didn't think I needed them in my life. I respected their decision and stayed away." Tricia looked up.

"I'm sorry Melissa. I didn't know." She continued with the salad.

"It's okay, I really don't mind talking about it. The only person I've ever talked to about the situation is Tarik. But we haven't talked about it in years. Phil is not the type to talk to about such problems. He always says that my parents will come around and accept us. It's been four years. I guess they're never going to accept my decision." Melissa took the celery and began dicing.

"Don't you miss your parents?" Tricia asked while seasoning the chicken.

"Of course I do. We were all so close at one time. I'm their only child."

"Well there's another thing we have in common." Tricia

said. "I'm an only child, too." They both looked at each other and smiled.

"Well at least you have Simone. You two are just as close as sisters are. Tricia's smile disappeared at the mentioning of Simone's name. Melissa noticed the look on Tricia's face.

"You two still aren't speaking huh?"

"No. Simone is not one of my favorite people right now. As a matter of fact, that brings me to the question I want to ask." Melissa didn't know what to think. She looked at Tricia with raised eyes.

"Okay."

Tricia sat down in a chair opposite Melissa.

"I would like to know if you would be my maid of honor." Melissa was stunned. She never thought that this would be the question Tricia was going to ask. She just sat there for a minute with her mouth hung open. Tricia got up to check on the chicken. Melissa's eyes followed Tricia to the stove.

"Tricia, are you serious?" Tricia turned to look at her.

"I know that it's short notice but I have thought about this and I want you to be there. You are Tarik's best friend and you should be in our wedding. Not to mention that you have become a very good friend to me also."

"Tricia, it would be my pleasure to be your maid of honor. But you do realize that I look like a punching bag, right? The bruises on my face may not be gone in time." Melissa looked sad after she made her last statement. Tricia noticed the look and tried to perk her up.

"Melissa the wedding is in six weeks. Your face will be healed by then. If not, that's what they have make-up for."

"Well then, I accept. Tricia your wedding is in a little over a month, what are we going to do about the dress and shoes?" Tricia took the chicken out of the pan and sat it on the table.

"Don't worry about that. I think I have it figured out. Simone is just a little bigger than you are. We'll just go to the tailor and have him measure you to see how much he'll have to take it in." She sat down and began slicing the chicken. "I already called this morning to make an appointment for this afternoon if you feel up to it." Melissa gave a hearty laugh.

"You just knew that I would say yes, huh?"

Tricia smiled. "Well, I hoped you'd say yes. And since you did, it all worked out. Where are the plates?"

"Look in the cupboard over the sink." Tricia went to the cupboard to get the plates and she remembered that she never told Melissa about the window that she broke to get inside the house last week. She looked over at the window and noticed that it was no longer broken.

"Melissa, when did you get the window fixed?" Melissa turned to look at Tricia.

"What window?"

Tricia sat down and fixed their plates.

"I forgot to tell you that in order for me to get in here last week, I had to break the window. I cleaned the glass when Dr. Carter came to examine you. Melissa went to the door to look at the window. She touched the glass closest to the doorknob.

"This glass is brand new. But I didn't even know it was broken." Melissa looked at Tricia with questioning eyes.

"Well that's strange." Tricia said as she went back to the table. Melissa was on her way to the table when she realized that only one person could have had the door fixed. She stopped dead in her tracks and turned back around to look on the board by the fridge. Then she saw it. Phil had left her the information for where he would be. It read that he was in Chicago and would be there until Wednesday.

"Oh my god! Phil was here. He left me his hotel information in Chicago." Tricia tried to be enthusiastic for Melissa when she saw the look of excitement on her face. She went to where Melissa was standing and hugged her.

"That's great Melissa! Does it say when he'll be back?"

They went back to the table.

"He'll be home on Wednesday." She kept the paper in her hand the whole time she ate. Tricia needed answers from Melissa and she couldn't hold her tongue any longer.

"Melissa, can we talk for a minute? About Phil?" Melissa finished chewing the food in her mouth then looked up at Tricia.

"Of course. What's up?" Tricia put her fork down and took a deep breath.

"I don't want you to think that I'm tryna get all up in your business but why do you stay with Phil?" Melissa smiled.

"How long were you wanting to ask me that?"

"Well, every since Tarik told me that he hit you just before you two were married."

"Tricia, I know I seem like a fool to you. You may never understand why I put up with Phil. But I will try to explain to you how I see my husband. Phil loves me very much and I love him. He'll do anything for me. He provides for me very well. I have a job that I really don't need. I only work to have something to do while he's working and away on business. When we met, I had just broken up with a boyfriend of four years. Phil was there for me in every way possible. He showed me things that my ex never could. He's a little selfish when it comes to me. He wants me all to himself. I knew of his ways before we got married but I loved him enough to overlook those qualities. I thought once we got married he'd calm down." Tricia sat there in disbelief.

"Lissa if you don't mind me saying so, you sound like you have low self esteem. Like you don't think much of yourself." Melissa looked into Tricia's eyes.

"I had low self esteem when I first met Phil. But he helped me with that. Besides Tarik, Phil was my only friend. When Tarik met you, he didn't have too much time for me so I turned to my husband." Tricia looked at Melissa and felt embarrassed.

"Tricia I don't mean to make you feel uncomfortable but I'm just trying to make you understand why I stay with my husband. When Tarik was too busy to talk, I'd turn to Phil and he'd make me feel like he was going to fix everything. Like he'd make all of my problems go away. And for that I'll love him forever."

"Melissa, do you think that Phil molded you into the woman that he wants you to be instead of the woman that you are meant to be? You are more that just Phil's wife!" Melissa put her hands up in defense. "Tricia, I think that this conversation is getting ready to take a turn for the worst. You are a great friend but I don't want to listen to you lecture me about my relationship with my husband. So please, let's change the subject." Tricia looked defeated.

"I'm sorry Melissa. You know Simone accused me of the same thing a few months ago. I guess I do spend too much time criticizing instead of being a friend. The subject is closed." Tricia sighed. "So, how are you feeling? Is your foot alright?"

"I feel fine. I was just thinking about the shoes for the wedding. I'm not going to be able to get my foot into a pump."

"I know. I've thought about that too. That's why I've ordered you open-toed sling backs this morning. They need to measure your foot to see if any changes should be made."

"Girl you have thought of everything, huh?" Tricia wiped her face before she spoke.

"I haven't thought of a way to tell Simone that she's not in the wedding." Melissa was surprised.

"Tricia, you mean you haven't told her yet? What are you waiting for?" Tricia sighed heavily.

"The right time I guess."

"Well, when do you think is the right time?"

"I'll tell her today." Melissa looked at Tricia and silently thanked her maker that she wasn't in her shoes.

Chapter 28

M rs. Hobbs walked into her living room just as Tricia opened the door.

"Oh, hi Momma."

"Hey baby. Whatchu doin' here?" Tricia moved to the side for Melissa. Melissa limped to Mrs. Hobbs and gave her a kiss on the cheek.

"Hello Mrs. Hobbs."

"Hey baby. What happened to yo foot?" Tricia closed the door and went to the sofa.

"Momma, Melissa broke her toe when she bumped her foot on an end table." Mrs. Hobbs looked at Tricia with raised eyes that said she was not born last night.

"What brang you girls out here?"

"We just came from getting Melissa fitted for the dress and shoes." Mrs. Hobbs looked at Tricia.

"Oh. Is Melissa going to be one of the bridesmaids?" Melissa looked at Tricia, too.

"Tricia you didn't tell your mother?" Mrs. Hobbs sat on the recliner.

"Tell me what, Tricia?" Tricia took the seat next to Melissa on the sofa.

"Well, I asked Melissa to be my maid of honor momma."

"What about Simone?" Tricia pushed herself to the back of the sofa.

"I don't want Simone in my wedding momma." Mrs. Hobbs spoke softly. "Tricia, was what happened between you and Simone that bad as to where you don't want her in yo wedding?" Tricia glanced over her shoulder at Melissa, who was also waiting intently for an answer. "Yes momma, it was that bad. I'm not going into details but my friendship with Simone is over!" Mrs. Hobbs sighed heavily. "Well, when did you break the news to Simone and how did she take it?" Tricia hesitated. "I'm going to call her in a few minutes to tell her." "Tricia, why haven't you told that girl? She's going to be so hurt. You know she was over here earlier this week?" Tricia frowned and asked, "What did she want?" Mrs. Hobbs pushed the recliner back so her feet were propped up.

"She just wanted to talk that's all. She wanted me to talk to you and make you listen to her. She's real upset about the fight. I told her that I was not getting involved." Tricia cursed under her breath.

"Momma, does she still have the keys to the house?"

"Of course she does chile." Tricia looked at her mother like she was crazy.

"Why does she still have them?"

"Tricia this fight is between you and Simone. She is still like a daughter to me. Like I told her, she always welcome here." Tricia felt bad. She knew that her mother would never get between the two especially if she didn't even know what the fight was about.

"You're right, momma. I'm sorry." Tricia looked at Melissa. "Want something to drink?"

"I would love some water." Tricia went to the kitchen to get one glass of wine. She grabbed a beer for her mother. When she returned a few minutes later, she handed them their drinks and took a sip from hers.

"Well I'm going to call Simone now.

"Tricia stay calm and be nice." Mrs. Hobbs said. Tricia went into the kitchen and picked up the phone. She took a deep breath before she dialed the numbers. She wasn't sure what she would say to Simone but she had to get this over with.

• • •

Simone was sitting on the sofa trying to figure out how to get through to Tricia when the ringing telephone interrupted her thoughts. She reached over the arm of the chair. "Hello?"

"Hi Simone. It's Tricia. I need to talk to you."

"Hey Trish, I was just thinking about you. I really want to apologize." Tricia cut her off. "Simone, that's not why I called. Please let me say what I need to say."

"I'm sorry, Trish. Go 'head." Tricia took another deep breath.

"Simone, I've been thinking about us and I've decided that I cannot have you in my life right now." Simone jumped from the sofa. "What?" Tricia paced the kitchen. "Simone that's how I feel right now. And I think it's best if you weren't in the wedding."

"Tricia, what are you talking about? We're sisters. We have been best friends since we were nine. How can you just decide that you don't want me in your life after what *we* did."

"Simone this is too hard for me. I am not prepared to answer questions. I just wanted to let you know how I feel. Don't worry about any of the money that you've put into the wedding. I will give you all of it back in a few days." Simone was now standing in the middle of her living room.

"Tricia, how da hell can you just say we're not friends when the wedding is in a little over a month?" Tricia breathed hard into the phone.

"Simone I would also appreciate it if you stopped calling me. I don't have anything more to say to you." With that said, she hung up the phone. Simone was stunned. She knew Tricia was pissed but she never thought she would end the friendship. She was hurt. She sat down on the sofa and cried. She thought about what Tricia said and realized what hurt the most was not being in the wedding. Tricia and Simone had fantasized about the day when either of them would get married for as long as she could remember. How can Tricia not want her in the wedding? She wondered. Simone picked up the phone and dialed *69. Tricia answered the phone on the second ring. "Yes?" She said in her normal tone.

"Tricia, please think about this before you make a decision that you can't take back." Tricia looked at the phone and hung up without saying another word. She walked into the living room where Melissa was engaged in a discussion with Mrs. Hobbs.

"How did it go?" Melissa asked as soon as she saw Tricia.

"It went as well as could be expected. I guess."

"Tricia, what the hell does that mean?" Mrs. Hobbs asked. Tricia sat on an end table.

"Simone didn't take it well. I don't even know how I expected her to take the news but I had to tell her." She grabbed a tissue from the box next to her and began wiping the corners of her eyes. Mrs. Hobbs went to her daughter to comfort her. She stood directly in front of Tricia and hugged her. Tricia was smothered in her mother's bosom for a minute.

"Well Tricia, you made yo decision. Now you have to deal with it in yo own way." Tricia shook her head up and down.

"Yes momma, I know."

"Well I'm going to the salon, unless you need me to stay here." Tricia looked at her mother with red eyes and smiled.

"No Mommy. I'll be fine. You go and get your hair done. I'll be gone when you get back but I'll call you later." Mrs. Hobbs went upstairs to get her purse. She came back down and said goodbye to Melissa then headed out the door.

Chapter 29

S imone lay across the sofa crying. Kareem entered the apartment two hours later.

"Simone, what's wrong baby?" He inched his way down on the sofa next to her. She lifted her head and cried harder. Kareem took her into his arms and held her. Simone just let her man comfort her for the next thirty minutes or so. She pulled back from his embrace and looked him directly in the eyes.

"Tricia called me and told me that she doesn't want me to be in her wedding." Kareem was speechless. He had no idea what to say to Simone.

"Simone, what happened between you and Tricia? I wish you would just talk to me. Maybe I can help you fix it." She moved over to the edge of the sofa and frowned her face.

"Kareem, I just wish you'd stop asking me what happened. It's a woman thing and you wouldn't understand." Simone tried to sound as irritated as possible, hoping that Kareem wouldn't push the issue.

"Are you sure, Simone? 'Cause this not being in the wedding sounds like it's mad serious." Simone grabbed his hand as a gesture of truce.

"Kareem, Tricia and I will work this out. I'll just back off and give her some space. She'll come around." Kareem looked confused.

"Simone, was the fight yo fault? You make it sound like you

did something to her." Simone looked away nervously.

"No, Kareem. It was both of us. I guess Tricia took it more serious than I did." Kareem had a concerned look on his face. "Are we still *going* to the wedding?" Simone shook her head yes. "We're going! I'm just not going to be in it."

"You gonna be alright being there but not being in the wedding with all of y'all friends knowing that you were supposed to be a part of it?" Simone never thought about it like that. However, she was not going to miss this wedding for anything. She knew Tricia meant that she didn't want her at the wedding either but Simone refused to miss out completely.

"Kareem just make sure you're here on time to escort me. I'll be fine." She said sarcastically. She got up from the sofa and went into the kitchen. Simone just realized that she hadn't eaten anything all day. "Kareem, you want a sandwich?" He came out of the bedroom when he heard Simone. "Nah, that's alright. I'll just grab something while I'm out." Simone raised her eyebrows. "Where are you going? You just got here." Kareem sighed. "So what? I'm going out for a little while."

"Going out where?" Simone inquired. Kareem pulled out a chair from the table and sat down. "If you don't mind, I'm going to shoot some pool with the fellas." Simone opened the fridge and grabbed the lunchmeat. She turned to Kareem and smirked. "What's with the smirking?" Simone continued to make the sandwich. She didn't even look at him when she answered. "Nothing Kareem. I'm not in the mood to argue so go and have fun." She said sarcastically. She took her food back into the living room and watched TV while she ate. Kareem went into the bathroom to take a shower. Simone really didn't care where Kareem was going. She didn't want him to get suspicious about anything. She knew his days were numbered. She was finally going to kick his cheating ass to the curb. She decided to wait until after the wedding. She still needed him as her escort.

After Kareem left, Simone lay back on the sofa. Her mind drifted back to the night she and Tricia had the fight. She replayed the events in her head over and over again. She just couldn't understand why her mind wouldn't let the images go. Every time she thought back to her putting her head in between Tricia's legs, she got wet. She began to wonder if she was bisexual. She remembered the feeling she got when she heard Tricia moan out in pleasure. Simone slid her fingers inside of her pants. She began to play with the hairs on her pussy. She kept the image of Tricia's face in her head as she stuck a finger into her pussy. She rocked back and forth on the sofa until she couldn't take it anymore. She stood and pulled her pants down. Simone sat on the floor and opened her legs. She inserted one finger at a time until her entire hand was able to fit inside of her. She took her other hand and started rubbing her clitoris very gently. Her body started to rock faster as she called Tricia's name in ecstasy. Simone remained on the floor panting for the next ten minutes. She looked around the room and began to feel embarrassed. She gathered her things and went to take a shower.

Simone stared crying again as soon as she stepped into the shower. She realized that she wanted Tricia in a sexual way. She tried so hard to erase the memories from her head but she couldn't. Every time she thought of Tricia, she became aroused. Simone couldn't understand this feeling. As long as she'd been with Kareem, she never experienced such a feeling by just thinking about him.

Chapter 30

T arik opened his cell phone and dialed Melissa's number. She answered on the first ring.

"Phil?" she asked. Tarik immediately turned his face.

"No. It's Tarik."

"Oh hey hon. What's up?" Tarik pulled into a McDonalds drive-thru.

"You. So you hit it off with Tricia and then forgot about me?"

Melissa laughed. "Now you know I couldn't forget about you. We've just been busy trying to get me ready for the wedding."

"Hold on, Melissa." She could here Tarik talking to someone. "Ok, I'm back."

"Who were you talking to?"

"Oh, I'm in the drive-thru getting me something to eat. I'm going back to the office. I need to get everything ready and in order before the honeymoon."

"I know that's right!" she agreed. "So, how have you been?" She asked nervously.

"Good. Tricia's keeping me busy with the wedding though. She always has something for me to see or do. I didn't know it was going to be this much work getting married."

"Well, I could've told you that." Tarik pulled out of the drive-thru and headed back to his office building. He was a supervising computer technician with Mitsubishi for the past four years.

"Melissa, I have to get back to work but you and I are getting together on Friday for drinks." Melissa knew she couldn't let Tarik see her like this. "Tarik how about next weekend?"

"Melissa, you have been avoiding me for almost two weeks. We are getting together this Friday if I have to come out to your house and drag you by the hair!" Melissa laughed at Tarik's sarcasm. "Ok Lissa, I have to go. See you Friday." Melissa didn't have a chance to respond because Tarik hung up the phone. She sat on the bed and wondered how she was going to pull this off. She knew that before anything, she had to make up with her husband.

Phil was all set to return home to his wife. He sat on the hotel bed and waited for the bellboy to help with the luggage. He didn't know what to get Melissa. He knew that she could care less if he brought her anything. He just felt so guilty about what he'd done to her. Phil put is head down and wondered if Melissa was ok. He came home the day after it happened to find that Melissa wasn't there. He called the hospital where she worked and was told that she was out on an emergency leave of absence. He didn't know what to think. He decided not to cancel his trip to Chicago. He hoped that when he returned they could begin to repair their marriage. Phil decided right then and there that he would do right by Melissa. He loved her with all that he had. Phil gathered the few things that the bellboy couldn't and headed for the car. On the ride, he thought about all that he and Melissa had been through. She was always there for him no matter what. The hard times they encountered when he first started the clinic. She never complained about anything. She lost the relationship with her parents on the strength of her love for him. He was going to be the husband that Melissa deserved from this point on. He picked up the car phone and dialed his travel agent. Phil made open reservations for he and Melissa to go to Aruba. This would be a vacation that both of them needed. Phil laid his head against the seat and dozed off thinking about his wife.

Chapter 31

K areem slid from under Shelly and went to take a shower. Fifteen minutes later, she joined him. "Were you trying to sneak out of here?" she asked as she rubbed different parts of his body.

"No. Why would I have to sneak?" he responded as he pushed her away from him.

"What's that all about?" she asked referring to his attitude.

"I just got a lot on my mind, Shelly." She grabbed the soap and lathered it across her body.

"What, you're thinking about Simone for a change?" she asked sarcastically. Kareem looked at her and smiled.

"That would kinda fuck yo head up wouldn't it?"

"Kareem don't fucking play games wit' me." He turned his back to her and stood under the warm water.

"Don't ask the question if you really don't wanna know the answer." He stepped out of the shower and snatched a towel from a hook. He headed into the bedroom to get dressed. Kareem wondered about Simone and Tricia's fight. There was something that Simone was not telling him and he intended to find out what was going on. Shelly entered the room wrapped in a towel. She sat on the bed next to him.

"Kareem, why are you leaving?"

"I have to take care of something real quick." She looked

disappointed.

"Are you coming back?"

"Not tonight."

She let out a heavy sigh. She was getting tired of Kareem just coming to see her when he wanted to have sex. Kareem looked over at her and frowned.

"Shelly, I think we need to slow this thing down a little." She looked him in the eyes.

"What? What are you talking about?" she snapped, "You are getting just a little too serious for me. I'm in a relationship and I'm not looking for another one."

"You're in a relationship, huh? I can't tell." Kareem stood to get his boots.

"Shelly, we both knew that this wouldn't last. It was just something for us to do."

"So you think you can just use me until you get tired? What? Am I supposed to just let you walk away?" Kareem turned around to look at Shelly. She couldn't possibly be serious, he thought.

"Shelly, bring it down. We fuck, that's all! It's not that serious." Shelly went to her walk-in closet to find something to put on. With her back to him, she began speaking very slowly.

"Kareem, you know, I'm tired of muthafuckas like you coming into my life dogging me out. You can't see past ya dick. You not stupid! You knew that if we fucked long enough, feelings would get involved. Now you wanna just walk away with another notch on yo belt!" She stepped out of the closet with a pair of jeans and a sweatshirt. She began to get dressed. Kareem sat at her desk and stared at her. "It's not going to work this time. You are not about to dismiss me like I'm a piece of trash." Kareem frowned his face. She carefully reached under the bed to grab her sneakers. "You fucked with the wrong one this time. I'm not one of those other bitches you got that punk shit off on. If I lose out, then so will you. Get the fuck out! You said it's over right?" She pointed towards the door.

"Shelly, calm the fuck down!" He went over to her and got right in her face. "Yo, you talkin real slick. Hate the game, not me." He brushed past her through to the living room and grabbed his hat and looked back. "Don't start nuthin' you can't finish."

"Get the fuck out, Kareem!" He looked at her face. He saw that she was hurting.

"Bye love." He smiled and walked out. Shelly slammed the door behind him. She didn't think Kareem took what she said seriously. She would just have to show him that she wasn't playing. Shelly picked up the phone and dialed Kareem's house. She hung up the phone before anyone had a chance to answer.

Chapter 32

P hil walked through the front door of his house. He held the flowers close to his heart. He had no idea if Melissa would be there or not. He cursed himself for not calling while he was away. He did check his cell phone and found that she'd left him several messages. He put the key in and opened the door. Melissa was not in the living room. Phil carefully placed his suitcase on the floor and went into the kitchen. He looked around but didn't see Melissa. He crept slowly up the stairs to the bedroom. Melissa was lying in bed staring at the TV.

"Melissa?" Phil whispered as he peeked his head through the door. Melissa jumped at the sound of his voice.

"My goodness Phil you scared me." She said trying to sound as nonchalant as possible. Melissa felt something she'd never felt before. She had been in bed thinking for two days. It was time she introduced her husband to the new Melissa. "So, you finally decided to show up huh?" Phil did not expect this attitude that Melissa presented. He stepped into the room.

"Melissa, how are you, baby?" She turned on the bed to face him.

"Phil, please don't do this."

"Do what? I just asked how you were."

"Don't come back acting like you care. You left me on the floor half-dead. You didn't even bother to call and check on me. How was I supposed to get help?" The tears started to flow from her eyes. Phil sat beside her on the bed.

"Melissa, after what I did to you, I couldn't face you. I know you've heard this before but, I swear I am never going to hit you again." Melissa rolled her eyes at him. "Baby, I know that you have no reason to believe anything I'm saying to you but I've had plenty of time to think. I'm going to stop drinking. We both know that drinking is the cause of my actions." Melissa didn't know what to say. She had heard Phil's speech time and time again. She wanted to believe her husband. No, she *needed* to believe him. Melissa controlled her crying and went to the full-length mirror. When she stood, Phil saw her bandaged toe and turned his head. She noticed his actions.

"You can't even look at me, huh? This is the result of your handy work." She began to examine herself. She pointed to her ribs that were bandaged also. "See?" She put her right hand on her left shoulder. "See this bruise here?" Phil was speechless. He hadn't realized that so much damage was done. Melissa slid down the pajamas she was wearing. "Look at my legs Phil. There's no telling when I'll be able to wear a pair of shorts again. Oh, did you see my foot? I have a broken toe, too." Phil held his head in his hands and began to sob. Melissa moved in closer to the mirror. She rubbed her hands against her face. She didn't know what to expect from Phil but she was going to say what was on her mind. "Phil, look at my face! There's no reason my face should look like this." Tears rolled down her cheeks as she spoke. Phil stood behind Melissa and held her from behind.

"Melissa, I'm so sorry. I mean it from the bottom of my heart."

She stepped out of Phil's reach. She slowly turned around to face him.

"Phil, I can't take this anymore. I am not your punching bag! I am a good woman and a good wife to you. But if this is all you think of me then..." She pointed to her face then walked

over and sat on the bed. "Melissa, wait baby just calm down."
He begged. "Are you talking about walking out on me?" She
looked at Phil like he was stupid.

"Walking out? I think I'm being pushed out, Phil. You
don't need me. And I can't live like this anymore."

"Ok, Melissa just wait," Phil pleaded. He got down on his
knees in front of her. He lifted her head so that their eyes met.
"Melissa, I love you and I do need you. We can work this out.
We can go see a marriage counselor baby, ok?" Melissa cried
even harder.

"I've heard you say that before. You always find some reason to cancel. How can I be sure that you'll go through with
it this time?"

"Baby, I have been doing a lot of thinking while I was in
Chicago. I am going to do right by you. I feel so bad that it took
this to happen in order for me to realize what I have in you.
Now that I see clearly, I'm not giving up on us." Melissa wiped
the tears from her eyes. She walked over to the mirror. "Phil,
look what you did to me! I don't deserve this! I refuse to put
up with this any longer!"

Phil looked at Melissa with tears in his eyes. He'd never
heard Melissa raise her voice to him. He didn't know how to
respond. Phil felt like Melissa wasn't giving in this time. He
didn't know what to do.

"Lissa, Please, lets just talk about this before you do anything. I'm begging you baby, please? She didn't say anything.
Phil walked up to her and hugged her from behind. After a
while, He guided her to the bed to sit down. They spent the rest
of the night talking. Melissa got everything off her chest. She
finally introduced her husband to Mrs. Melissa Monroe. Phil
sat back and listened to her without interruption. He knew
that she needed to vent. She went on for hours telling him
how things were going to be different. She sat back and
thought about her life. She suddenly realized that marriage

made her lose touch with who she really is. She never really experienced being Melissa Evans. When Phil made her his wife, she never looked back.

Phil woke up and headed out of the bedroom.
"Where are you going?"
He looked back over his shoulder. "I'm going to the kitchen honey. I'll be right back."
"Oh. Ok." Melissa went into the bathroom and turned on the shower. She then went to the armoire to get another pair of pajamas to sleep in. She stepped into the shower and relaxed as soon as the hot water hit her skin. She stood under the water for a few more minutes. She thought more about her marriage. She couldn't believe that Phil offered to see a marriage counselor. She'd been trying to get him to see a counselor for two years. Melissa would do anything to save her marriage. She wasn't sure if Phil noticed or not but she had no intentions of leaving. She needed to make Phil realize that he was out of control. She washed up a couple of times and got out of the shower. Melissa was surprised when she walked into the bedroom. Phil had turned down the lights and lit candles. There was a Will Downing cd playing in the background. He even set up two trays of food. Phil walked in the room carrying a bottle of champagne and two glasses. He sat on the bed next to Melissa and hugged her.
"I love you, Lissa. There's nothing I wouldn't do for you." Phil escorted her to the top of the bed. He placed a tray of food in front of her and poured her a glass of champagne. He went to his side of the bed and set up his own tray. They ate their meal in silence. When they were done, Phil removed the trays and snuggled next to his wife in the bed.
"Melissa, I'd like to know what happened. How you made it out of here. If you feel like talking about it." She looked at her husband for what seemed like an eternity. She proceeded

in telling Phil exactly what happened. Phil squeezed her tightly. "Ouch, Phil! Be careful with my arm." Phil eased his grip on Melissa and apologized. Melissa turned her body to face him. "Phil, it was so embarrassing to let anyone see me like this. I heard everything you said tonight. But I need you to hear something. This is the last time you'll ever put your hands on me. I will not let you do this to me again!" She said as she pointed to different bruises on her body. "I am very serious Phil. You'll never hurt me like this again!" Phil noticed a change in Melissa's voice after her last statement. He'd never heard Melissa so serious. He knew that she meant what she'd said. Phil positioned himself on his side.

"Melissa, I agree with you. I told you. I will never put my hands on you to hurt you again. I mean it." She looked at her husband and more tears welled in the corners of her eyes. Phil gently held Melissa and they fell asleep in that position.

Chapter 33

Phil planned to take a shower before Melissa woke. He called the clinic to make sure things were in order with all his patients. He also told his assistant Alicia that he would be out this morning. She informed Phil of the many times that his wife phoned. Phil assured her that everything was ok. He hung up and went to take a shower. Melissa woke just when Phil was getting back into the bed.

"Where've you been?"

"I took a shower." She inched over to lie on her husband's chest. Phil kissed the top of Melissa's head. He rubbed up and down her arms being very careful not to hurt her. Melissa knew what was about to happen. She was horny as hell but didn't want to make the first move. Phil noticed that Melissa didn't reject his advances so he continued. He lifted her shirt and massaged her breasts. She moved her body in motion with Phil's rhythm. Phil slid his hand inside her pajamas. Melissa squirmed. She began to caress his penis. Phil jerked at the touch of Melissa's hands. He kissed her hard on the mouth. He eased over her body. Phil used his tongue to massage her nipples. He squeezed her breasts together and licked them both simultaneously. Melissa moaned in pleasure. Phil went down a little further and licked her navel. His hands played down south while his mouth explored up north. Melissa could no longer stand the agony. She guided Phil's head down a little further. Phil opened her pussy with his fingers and licked her clit nice and slow. Melissa lost control and began pumping her body up and down careful not to hurt her ribs. Phil teased her like this for a while longer. She kept her hand on his head to assure pleasure. Phil slowed his pace and looked up at Melissa. He took pride in seeing the look of pleasure on her face. Phil went back down and fucked her with his tongue. This drove Melissa wild. She didn't seem to notice the pain as she lifted her ass each time Phil stuck his tongue in her nest. As Phil worked his way to her nipples, he planted soft kisses over every spot on her body. He sucked gently on her neck and finally kissed her passionately. Melissa grabbed Phil's seven-inch dick and slid it inside of her. Phil was careful to move nice and slow. He didn't want to hurt her bruised body. He looked down at her face as he made love to his wife. She was beautiful with her hair thrown all over the pillow. She made the sexiest faces. It turned him on to watch her cum. Melissa wrapped her legs around Phil's waist and let him pump in and out of her. She was having the most electrifying orgasm. She moaned louder with each stroke until she finished. Phil smiled and kissed her cheek. He could feel an orgasm on the way. He deep stroked Melissa a few times then collapsed on top of her. "Phil you have to get up. My ribs are still a little sore. Phil rolled over and placed Melissa in his arms. They were asleep within minutes.

Chapter 34

S imone decided that she needed to buy a dress to wear for the wedding. She got dressed and went shopping. She drove to Woodbridge Mall and found a small boutique. While she was browsing, a sales associate asked her if she needed help. Simone looked at the woman and smiled.

"As a matter of fact, you can help me." She dug inside her purse and found a picture with the dress she was supposed to wear to the wedding. "I need you to help me find a dress in this color." She said holding the picture in front of the associate. She read the associate's nametag and whispered. "Carmen, the dress I wear must be fierce. I need to show off all of my 'assests' if you know what I mean." Carmen looked at Simone and smiled.

"Well then my dear, get ready. I have a selection that I think you are going to love." Simone followed Carmen to a waiting area. Carmen returned with three dresses that were almost the identical color of the dress in the picture. The first dress was beautiful. It had spaghetti straps and a split in the back. The next dress was also gorgeous. It had a split on each side and one spaghetti-strap. The third dress caught Simone's eye. It was intriguing. It was a strapless number with a split on the right side. It was cut low in the front and it came with a shawl. This was the dress Simone would wear to the wedding.

"Carmen, I think I'm in love. This is the dress I want right here. Now, please tell me that you have it in a size six." Carmen looked at the tag on the dress and frowned.

"This is an eight." Simone cursed a few times before she spoke.

"Well Carmen, do you think your store could have this dress tailored to fit me in three weeks?" Carmen smiled. "Of course we could. It would only have to be taken in a few inches. I will take your measurements and send the dress out today." Simone smiled with pleasure.

"That would be great. You are a lifesaver, girl." Carmen disappeared to the back to return the other dresses. Simone got undressed in the fitting room and waited to get her body measured.

An hour later Simone was headed to the shoe stores. She went to a couple of stores but didn't see the right shoe to complement the outfit. She stopped at a pretzel time stand and ordered a salted pretzel. As she turned to get money from her purse, she caught a glimpse of the perfect shoe. It was an opened-toed, back-out, high heel. It had a very thin line of glitter across the top strap. She left the stand without paying and went inside the store. A sales assistant rushed right to her and asked if she needed assistance. Simone went to the window and asked the man if he had the shoe in a size nine. The man went to the back and returned with two boxes.

"Unfortunately, I don't have a nine but I did bring you an eight and a half and a nine and a half just in case. Simone sat in one of the chairs. She removed her sneaker and looked around for a box of trial socks. The sales assistant handed her one from the box next to him on the counter.

"Let me see the nine and a half please." He removed the right shoe from the box and handed it to Simone. She examined the shoe a few more seconds before trying it on. "I really hope this shoe fits. It is the only shoe that I've seen all day to match this dress." She slid her foot into the shoe and stood.

"Well, it feels alright." She walked to a mirror and viewed her feet from another angle. Do you think you could order my size within the next two weeks?" She asked as she sat back in the chair.

"I'm sorry ma'am but this shoe is no longer in stock. These are all that's left." Simone sighed.

"It's a little big but I guess I'll manage." She removed the shoe from her foot. "Wrap 'em up. I'll take 'em." Simone paid for the shoes and left the mall feeling good about the rest of the day. She decided to go to the gym and get a quick workout in before it got too late. She did not want to see or have any run-ins with Tricia until the wedding. She knew Tricia went to the gym on Saturday mornings. To avoid running into her, she'd go today.

Chapter 35

S helly pulled her car out of the mall at the same time as Simone. She had been following her all day. When she saw Simone pull into the parking lot to the gym, she knew it was time to get started with her plan. She watched Simone go inside the gym before she got out of her car. Shelly went across the street to Modell's and purchased a warm-up suit. She already had sneakers on. She crossed the street and entered the gym. She spotted Simone on the treadmill as soon as she walked in. Shelly went over to the empty treadmill next to Simone. Simone looked over at Shelly and smiled a hello. Shelly couldn't get the treadmill working. After a few times of failing, she asked Simone if she could help her get started. Simone jumped off her machine and introduced herself.

"Hi, I'm Simone. She held out her hand for a shake.

"I'm Shelly. Nice to meet you." Simone pressed a few buttons and got Shelly started on her workout.

"Thank you so much. Simone right?"

"Yep. You're welcome." Simone went back to her machine and continued to walk the treadmill. Shelly sensed that Simone was in a good mood so she struck a conversation with her.

"So, do you come here often, Simone?" Simone looked over at Shelly.

"I sure do. Every other Saturday with a friend of mine." Shelly smiled.

"Well, it's my first time here so I don't know how to work the equipment." Simone stopped her machine and stood next to Shelly.

"Why don't you come to the step class? It starts in ten minutes." Shelly stopped her machine.

"That sounds like fun. Where is it held?" Simone looked over in the direction of the classroom and pointed.

"Right in there." Shelly stepped off the treadmill.

"Where can I get a bottle of water?" Simone led her to the snack area.

"It's kinda expensive. I usually bring my own, but since I just came from the mall and this was a last minute decision..." She shrugged her shoulders. The two ladies stood in line and both bought a bottle of water. When they left out of the step class, both were exhausted and sweaty.

"Well that's it for me. He wore me out in that class." Simone said between deep breaths.

"I had enough too." Shelly said between heavy breaths. She was walking around in circles trying to catch her breath.

"Where are the showers?" she asked. Simone stood and wiped the sweat from her forehead with a towel.

"Come on, I'm going there right now." As they headed to the showers, they made plans to go to the salad bar for lunch.

"I'll meet you out front in fifteen minutes." Simone said as she headed to her locker.

"That's cool. It's not going to take me long." Shelly responded.

During lunch, Simone talked to Shelly about Tricia. She told her that they were good friends but having a disagreement right now. She told Shelly that she's giving Tricia some cooling off space. Shelly was surprised that Simone revealed so much about herself. She knew about her relationship with Kareem within the hour. Shelly discovered that Simone was getting tired of Kareem's shit and was planning on dumping him in a very short time. Simone also explained that Kareem suspected something was up so he's being extra nice and loving towards her.

"Oh my goodness! I'm just sitting here telling you all of my business. I just feel like I've known you for ever." Simone said between laughs.

"It's okay. I really don't mind listening. You probably just miss yo girl and needed someone to talk to." Shelly suggested.

"You're right. I do tell Tricia everything. And since we haven't been speaking, I've been keeping all of this to myself." Simone had a look of depression on her face. Shelly didn't know what to say but she knew she couldn't go through with her plans now. Simone was not at all what she expected. Simone was really nice and didn't deserve to hear what Shelly was prepared to tell her. Simone seemed to be so in love with Kareem. She was just getting tired of his ways. Shelly knew first hand what Simone was going through. She too was in love with Kareem. She decided that her plans would change. She knew that she didn't want to be with Kareem knowing how he treats Simone. She also wanted to hurt Kareem for the way he used her. Shelly decided to befriend Simone. She would make sure that Simone kicked his sorry ass to the curb.

Shelly and Simone stood outside the deli. They'd just finished lunch and were talking about getting together to hit the club next weekend. Simone scribbled her number on a piece of paper and handed it to Shelly. Shelly did the same for Simone. The two decided that they would work out together every other Friday after work. They said their goodbyes and headed in different directions to their cars.

Chapter 36

Melissa woke to a ringing phone. She reached over to answer. "Hello?" She asked in a groggy voice.

"Don't tell me you're still sleeping girl?" Tricia laughed.

"Hey Tricia. What's up?" She asked as she sat up in the bed.

"I was just wondering if you can get away for a few? The dress and shoes are here and I want you to try them on." A big smile crept over Melissa's face. She was so excited about being a part of the wedding.

"What time should I be there?" Melissa asked.

"If you're not busy, I was hoping you could come now. That way we can have a rehearsal while you're here. The other girls are on the way to Moms' house." Melissa looked over at Phil who was looking at her with questioning eyes. She smiled at her husband.

"Sounds like a plan to me. See you in a few."

"Melissa." Tricia called out before they hung up the phone.

"Yeah?"

"Do you need a ride?"

"Girl I've told you that I'm ok. I can drive myself around. My body is healing real nice but thanks for the offer."

"Well excuse me for caring miss thang. Bye." Tricia said and hung up the phone. Melissa laughed and put her phone back in its cradle. She got out of the bed and went to her walk-in closet. She pulled out a long beige Donna Karen skirt with a matching long sleeved shirt. She placed the clothing on the bed and went to her armoire to get under garments. "What's going on, Melissa?" Phil asked as he sat up in the bed.

"Oh. I'm going out for a while. Hope you don't mind." She said as she went into the bathroom to turn on the shower water.

"Well, I thought that we would spend the day together baby." Melissa went over to the bed and sat next to her husband.

"Phil, did I tell you Tricia asked me to be her maid of honor?" She asked in a thrilled voice. "She wants me to come over to try on my dress and shoes. Then we're going to have a rehearsal." Phil didn't know how to react. He wanted to tell Melissa that she was not going anywhere but it was only his first day back. He remembered the look in her eyes when Melissa told him that he would never put his hands on her again. He decided not to contest her plans.

"Well, I do need to get some things done today. So I guess I'll see you when you get back, huh? About what time would that be?" he asked.

"I'm not sure how long this is going to last, but I'll call you to let you know what time to expect me." She went into the bathroom and closed the door. Phil was not used to Melissa's new attitude. Melissa always asked him if it was ok if she went and did whatever. Now, she didn't seem to care what he thought. She was going and that was all to it. Phil got up and made the bed. He began gathering his toiletries for a shower. Melissa came out of the bathroom with her towel wrapped around her. She took Phil by the hand.

"Come sit down with me for a minute." Phil followed Melissa to the bed. "I know that you didn't approve of my friends before you left. But I feel the need to explain this to you.

I already told you that Tricia was the one who helped me through this whole ordeal. She was right here by my side when I needed someone. I'll always be grateful to her for that. She and I have become very good friends and I really wish that you would accept that. I have gotten used to having a girlfriend in my life again. I am not going to turn my back on her because you want me all to yourself."

"Melissa, I am willing to do whatever it takes to make you happy. If it means accepting your friends, then that's what I'll do. I guess I should get to know them before I judge them," he said as he hugged his wife. Melissa welcomed his hug but didn't know what to think. Phil was never this open when it came to meeting any of her friends.

"Phil, I really appreciate this. Thank you." Melissa went to her vanity to do her hair.

"You don't have to thank me sweetie. I am dedicated to making you happy from now on." She looked in her mirror and smiled at Phil. "I'm glad you feel that way because this means that you and Tarik are going to have to get along since Trish and I are so close." Phil looked at Melissa and tried to smile. "Whatever it takes, baby."

He went into the bathroom and took a shower. Melissa continued to get dressed. When she was through, she carefully applied make-up to her face to hide the swelling. She opened the bathroom door and told Phil that she'd call him later.

Chapter 37

T arik walked into the bedroom and saw Tricia staring out the window.

"What's on your mind Boo?" The sound of his voice made Tricia jump.

"I didn't even hear you come in. I was just sitting here thinking that in two weeks, we're going to be married." Tarik smiled.

"I know. I've been counting the days too. I can't believe that we're almost there. It seemed like we had so much time to plan but now that it's so close, I'm asking where did the time go?" He sat in a chair facing her.

"Don't tell me you are having cold feet." Tricia teased.

"Not at all. I'm more excited about this day than you." Tricia smiled and shook her head.

"No, maybe as much as me but not more than me. I can't wait to become Mrs. Tarik Hammond. This is all Simone and I talked about when you and I first met. I knew you were the one." Tarik looked into Tricia's eyes.

"Trish, why won't you make amends with Simone before we get married? After all the four of us have been through, I can't see us getting married without her by our side." Tricia looked at her fiancé long and hard.

"Tarik, please don't do this now. We've already discussed how I feel about Simone being in my wedding. You said you were cool with it so why the change of heart?" Tarik leaned back in the chair.

"Tricia this is *our* wedding, not yours alone. I just don't understand what made you so upset that you don't want your best friend by your side. Like you said, you and Simone have been talking about this day for years."

"Tarik, could we please just drop it? Damn! I don't want to talk about Simone!"

"Well, will you at least tell me what happened between you two?"

"No. I will not!" she said as she went into the kitchen. Tarik followed her.

"Tricia, I don't want to upset you or push the issue but Kareem came to see me the other day. He asked me if I knew what was going on between you and Simone." Tricia stopped dead in her tracks.

"What? Since when does he care?"

"Tricia, the three of you grew up together. It's only natural for him to be concerned that the two of you are not speaking especially when it affects him."

"Well this does not affect Kareem."

"Actually, it affects Kareem and me. You and Simone stopped speaking to each other. Neither one of you tells us why and you expect us to understand and let it be? That's not fair and you know it! The two of you were inseparable and now this. No matter how much it hurts us to see you two in pain, you still won't tell us what happened?"

"Tarik, I have to meet Melissa at Mom's house in a few. It's not fair that I show up with an attitude. So, I'm leaving now and I'll see you at the church."

"Tricia, I know you're not gonna just walk out in the middle of a discussion?"

"There is no discussion. I told you that I didn't want to talk about it but you keep pushing and pushing. I can see where this is going, so I'm leaving." She went into the bed-room to put on her sandals.

"You know the one thing I can't stand about you Tricia is your selfishness. It always has to be your way or no way right? You're just gonna walk out because right now it's an inconvenient time for you to discuss this huh?"

"Selfish? You're calling me selfish?" She laughed. "Tarik I'm not even going to feed into that bullshit! I'll see you later." She slammed the door on her way out.

Chapter 38

Tricia stood on her mother's porch and peeked through the window. She rang the bell instead of using her key. Mrs. Hobbs looked at the door and saw Tricia standing there.

"Why didn't you use yo key, girl? I know you saw me on the phone." Tricia entered the house and sat on the sofa across from her mother.

"I'm just respecting your house. I saw you sitting here so I didn't want to barge in." Mrs. Hobbs ended her phone conversation with a laugh and hung up the phone.

"Well, that's the reason you have keys. So I don't hafta get up to let you in."

"Momma, I didn't feel right barging into your house when I saw you sitting right there." Tricia took off her shoes and sat Indian style on the sofa. "Did any of the girls call, momma?"

"Um, as a matter of fact, Chelsea called and said she'd meet y'all at the church because she has to take her son to his father." Tricia went and picked up the bag she left by the door. She pulled out the shoes and laid them across the sofa.

"I sure hope the swelling in Melissa's foot went down."

Mrs. Hobbs smirked. "I hope that was the last time she let that man beat her like that."

Tricia looked surprised. "Momma, how did you know?"

"Tricia, I was not born yesterday. I had a little talk with Melissa the last time she was here. I really hope she heard what I was saying. It's a shame that her self esteem is so low."

"I know. I've tried to talk to her about it too but she's blinded by love." Mrs. Hobbs shook her head.

"Well unfortunately, some things have to be learned from experience. Who are we to tell her she deserves better? She needs to believe that on her own." The doorbell rang as soon as Tricia was about to speak.

"I'll get it Momma." Tricia looked through the curtain and saw Melissa standing there. She opened the door and stepped to the side to let her in.

"Hello Mrs. Hobbs. Hey Trish." Melissa said as she sat in the lazy boy recliner.

"Well it's about time you made it." Tricia said with her hands on her hip.

"I thought I was going to have to file a missing persons report."

Melissa laughed. "I am not that late. Anyhow, it looks like I'm the only one here."

Mrs. Hobbs walked towards the kitchen. "Oh Tricia, please! Melissa, she just got here herself." Tricia laughed.

"The nerve of you to accuse me of being late when you just arrived yourself." They both laughed.

"Well look what I have for you!" Tricia squealed. She handed Melissa the shoes. "Go ahead and try them on girl." Melissa removed one of her sandals.

"Tricia, these shoes are exquisite." She slid her foot into one of the shoes.

"Well, how does it feel?" Tricia asked.

"It's a tad bit tight but I'll manage."

Tricia sighed at the thought of anything going wrong at the wedding.

"Are you sure Melissa cause we could always get you something out of a shoe store and match it up with the dress." Melissa looked up with a smirk on her face.

"Tricia please! If that's what you wanted then you would not have ordered these special made shoes that match the dress to the tee. Don't worry honey I'll be fine. As long as I get through the ceremony, I can take them off at the reception."

Tricia smiled at Melissa.

"I really appreciate that girl." The doorbell rang and Mrs. Hobbs ran out of the kitchen to answer. "Momma it's probably some of the girls. You know I could let them in. Are you expecting someone?" Mrs. Hobbs blushed. "Girl mind yo own business." Then she went back into the kitchen.

Tricia opened the door to let the ladies inside. They all rode together in Sabrina's Durango. Everyone said hello and took a seat. Tricia stood in the middle of the floor. "Ladies, I have good news. The shoes and dresses are here. I'll let you guys try them on in a minute but first I need to tell you all something." Tricia looked nervous. Melissa wondered what Tricia was going to say. "I know that you all have probably already heard through the grapevine, but I feel you need to hear it from me. Simone and I are not on speaking terms at the moment. She's not going to be in the wedding." Most of the women had known that Tricia and Simone were not speaking but they didn't know it was this serious. Sabrina, a friend from college was the first to speak.

"Tricia, what's going on? You and Simone are sisters. What do you mean she's not in your wedding?"

Tricia held her hands up in defense.

"Wait a minute y'all. I am not going into details about what caused Simone and my friendship to end, but I do want to let you know that I've asked Melissa to be my maid of honor and she's agreed." All the women looked at Melissa and congratulated her. Melissa felt a negative vibe from Sabrina. She would be sure to ask Tricia about her when the time was right. Melissa smiled and thanked the ladies in return.

"Well now that that's over, we can try on these dresses and

shoes.

"Where's Chelsea?" Sabrina asked.

"Oh she's going to meet us at the church." Melissa offered.

Sabrina rolled her eyes to the back of her head as if to say, '*who asked you?*" Melissa mingled with the other women and helped them with their dresses. After another two hours of fitting, the women headed to the church.

"Melissa, do you mind if I ride with you?" Tricia asked. "I do not feel like driving right now." Melissa grabbed her purse.

"Sure. Let's go."

Chapter 39

The ladies gathered in front of the church.

"I see Reverend Gaines is already here." Tricia said.

"Yep." Sabrina said as she looked at his parked car in the pastor's parking spot. Tricia looked around to see if she saw Tarik's car. They went inside and spotted Chelsea sitting in the front pew on her cell phone. Chelsea was just ending her conversation when she looked up and saw the girls.

"Hey girl, I bought your dress and shoes for you to try on." Tricia said as she sat next to her.

"Oh, they're back already?"

"Yep. They all tried theirs on and they look hot girl!" All the ladies laughed at Tricia's imitation.

"Do I have time to try this on now?" Tricia looked around and still didn't see Tarik and his boys.

"I guess so. Tarik and 'em ain't here yet. Let's go in the choir room." They started walking towards the room. Tricia looked back. "Come on y'all, Chelsea's gonna try on her dress." The women went off to the room.

Tarik and his cousin Will walked into the church but didn't see anyone.

"Where are they?" Will asked.

"Well they're here somewhere cause there's all their things." Tarik said as he pointed to the front pew. Four other men entered the church five minutes later. Reverend Gaines came out and stood in front of the podium.

"Where are the ladies?" Just then Melissa walked out from the back.

"Here we are," she smiled. She noticed Tarik and tried not to limp.

"Hey babe, what's up? Where's my bride to be?" Melissa smiled.

"They're coming. They were helping Chelsea with her dress."

"Oh good, you guys made it." Tricia said as she walked from the back carrying the dress. There was a little attitude in her voice. She was still upset with Tarik about their earlier discussion. Reverend Gaines cleared his throat and asked the ladies to take their positions. The wedding party went through three rehearsals before Tricia was satisfied everyone knew their role.

"Tricia, you want me to follow you back to your mother's house?" Tarik asked. She looked at him and rolled her eyes.

"No Tarik, the girls and I are going back to tie up a few loose ends. But I'll be home in a couple of hours." Tarik stared at Tricia in disbelief. He was now positive that she was still upset with him. Will overheard the end of their conversation.

"Don't worry Trish, we'll keep him company until you get home." Tarik looked at Will with his eyebrows raised. "Let's be out." Will smiled. Tarik looked at Tricia for a moment then walked towards five other guys. Tarik stopped in front of Melissa.

"It looks like we're going to have to get together another time."

Melissa smiled. "That's cool. We can catch up next week sometime."

"You're not getting off that easily Melissa. We will get

together tomorrow. So what's a good time for you?" Tarik waited for an answer.

"Since I'm not working right now, you can come by some-time during the day." She paused. "Oh wait, you're working tomorrow, right?" Tarik noticed that Melissa never looked him in the eyes.

"Well I can always go in a couple of hours late. It is Saturday. So I'll be there around 8:30." Melissa looked in the opposite direction. "That's a plan. Phil won't be here so I'll see you then," she said as she walked off towards the women.

Chapter 40

Tarik was not in the mood to hang with the fellas. "Tarik man, what's up? You've been holding your head down every since we left the church." Will said as they got out of the car.

"Nah, I'm alright. I just didn't plan on hanging out tonight."

"Well, just stay and have a drink or two." Will smiled then opened the door to the bar.

"Will, is this place even open?" Tarik felt the wall for the light switch. A crowd of men yelled surprise as he turned on the lights.

"Welcome to your bachelor party cuz'!" Tarik looked around the bar at all of the familiar faces.

"Damn, I haven't seen most of y'all in a while." He walked around the bar shaking hands and giving the brutha hug.

"Yo, Tarik, we got you good man. You didn't have a clue." Will said as he opened a bottle of beer.

Tarik laughed. "Yeah, y'all got me." He began to relax and mingle with his friends. The fellas sat around the bar a few more hours drinking and talking about women.

"Tarik, are you starting to feel like this is a mistake man?" Sean asked. Sean and Tarik shared a dorm room in college.

"Nah. This is it. Tricia is definitely the one I was meant to be with." Tarik said with a smile.

"That's what you say now. When I first married Mia, I felt the same way. But after seven years, I should have thought with my big head instead of my little head." Everyone laughed.

"Are you saying that you don't love her man?" Tarik asked as he turned his barstool towards Sean.

"Nah... I'm not saying I don't love her. It's just that things take a turn for the worse when you put that ring on their finger and give 'em yo last name. They become yo moms instead of yo wife." Most of the guys nodded in agreement with Sean.

"Tricia is not like that." Tarik said. Will let out a loud chuckle. Tarik spun around to face him. "Now Will, you know that me and Tricia are friends before anything. Our getting married ain't gonna change that." Sean led the fellas in the jokes this time.

"Now Tarik, we boys right?" a tall guy named Hunter said, "So don't think that we're trying to discourage you from marrying Tricia. We just wanna let you know that it changes after the wedding. So don't expect it to be all good."

"That's what's up." Sean added. Tarik looked around the bar.

"Y'all full of shit." Everyone laughed.

"Ok man. Just don't say we didn't warn you." Hunter said as he grabbed another beer.

"Alright fellas, it's time to let Tarik enjoy the last of his freedom before Tricia claim that, too." Will said as he turned down the lights. Two women dressed in lingerie stepped on the stage. One woman was about 5'9" and 145 lbs. She was wearing a blue garter with the matching thong. She had on a lace bra and blue high-heeled pumps. She made her way to the pole in the middle of the stage. She stood with her back to the men. She tilted her head so that she could see the men from the corner of her eye. Janet Jackson's 'I Get So Lonely' blasted from the speakers. The dancer turned to face the men and posed a few times before she went into her act. She did a slow seductive strip-tease dance. The men were in awe. They were amazed that she was so flexible. Towards the end of the song, the woman moved closer to the men. She teased a few of them with a scarf. The men were screaming and drooling like dogs. Tarik sat back and watched the woman do her thing. She spotted him and moved in his direction. She bent down and pulled him onto the stage with her. Tarik was a little reluctant at first but then he relaxed and got with the program. She removed his shirt and played with his nipples a bit. She turned her back to Tarik and did a slow grind with the music. He grabbed her by the hands and spun her around to face him. The men cheered and barked for Tarik to do more. The stripper undid Tarik's pants and got on her knees. He grabbed her by the hair and stepped back. She looked up at him like he was crazy. Will yelled over the music, "What's up, man? Why you tripping?" Tarik looked at Will and shook his head.

"It's not my thing man. I ain't tryna fuck her. I was just having a little fun." Kareem climbed on stage and gave Tarik a tug. Tarik climbed down and Kareem took his place. The stripper undid Kareem's pants and used her mouth to find his dick. Kareem grabbed the back of her head to guide her. She began to suck his dick right there on stage. Tarik went to the bar to get a drink. He asked for a shot of Hennesy. The other men all crowded around the stage and watched. After they witnessed Kareem's orgasm, they argued about who was next. Tarik shook his head in disgust. He sat there and debated about kicking Kareem's ass. He has a good woman at home and he's out here letting some stripper suck his dick. Tarik just sat there thinking.

The second stripper approached Tarik. She was very tall standing at least six feet. She stood in front of Tarik and started to give him a lap dance. She moved on beat with the song that was playing. Tarik was very impressed that the woman was able to keep beat with the fast song. The stripper stepped back and begun to remove the few clothes she was wearing. Tarik was not feeling this bachelor party. He did not expect this. He didn't mind having a little fun and dancing with strippers, but he was not willing to have sex with them. Will noticed the second stripper dancing in front of Tarik and went over to the bar where they were. He asked the woman to excuse herself. He sat on a stool next to Tarik.

"What's wrong man, why you trippin'? I thought you would come out and enjoy yourself and have a little fun before you take that trip down the aisle."

"Will man, I don't know why you can't understand that I love Tricia and I'm not about to fuck some stripper in a bar just to prove to y'all niggas that I'm cool. Now if y'all wanna sit here and do that shit, then fine. But you know I'm not that nigga. I'm out, man." Tarik left Will standing by the bar.

Chapter 41

Tricia went straight to the kitchen to get some wine. The ladies all sat in the living room and got comfortable. Melissa chose the recliner and leaned back to elevate her feet. Tricia returned and gave each woman a glass.

Sabrina stood. "Let's have a toast to Tricia and Tarik. May they always be happy!" Every one of the ladies cheered. They drank three more bottles of wine. Melissa got up and went to the kitchen. She picked up the phone and started to dial her house. Tricia swung open the door.

"Everything ok girl?" Melissa turned around startled.

"Yeah. I was just calling home. Phil came back on Wednesday." She smiled. "I just wanted to let him know that I'll be home in a couple of hours." Tricia raised her eyebrows.

"You sure it's ok, Lissa? Do you need to leave now?" Melissa assured Tricia that it was ok.

"I just need to call Phil so he won't worry." Tricia was backing out of the kitchen.

"Ok."

Melissa proceeded to dial the number. Phil answered on the first ring.

"Hey baby." Melissa sang.

"Hi honey. You ok?" Phil asked.

"Yep, I'm fine. Just wanted to let you know that I'd be home in about two hours. We just came from the church and we're finishing up some small details." Phil bit his tongue and smiled.

"I understand. I have a ton of paperwork to tackle before I go to the office in the morning. I'll be downstairs in the office when you get in." Melissa smiled.

"I love you, Phil. Thank you for trying to understand. I know how hard this is for you."

"Melissa, baby don't worry about it. Have fun with your friends and I'll see you later. Ok?"

"Ok Phil, I'll see you in a bit."

Melissa entered the living room and smiled at Tricia.

"Everything ok?" Tricia asked.

"Perfect!" Melissa responded. She took her position back on the recliner. The ladies discussed more details about the wedding. Tricia grabbed her glass and stood.

"I would like to take this time to thank all of you for making this wedding that much easier for me. I am so grateful to have you all in my life. I really appreciate everything that you're doing. I especially want to thank Melissa, for accepting the responsibility of being my maid of honor at the last minute. You are truly a lifesaver." Tricia raised her glass and all the ladies cheered. Melissa looked at Tricia and mouthed, you're welcome then smiled.

"Ladies, can I interrupt just one more time? Tricia, as the maid of honor, I am responsible for the bachelorette party. I'm so sorry that it's not enough time for me to plan a nice one for you. However, I will be having a dinner party for you at my house next weekend. Ladies I hope you all can attend because this will probably be the last time for a while Tricia will have dinner with you." Everyone laughed. Tricia threw a pillow at Melissa then laughed along with everyone else.

"That's fine, Melissa. Just promise me that you won't have any strippers. I have all the stripper I need at home." The ladies continued to laugh.

"A stripper? Tricia, please, that is hardly my style." Melissa winked. "But we're going to have fun anyhow."

Chapter 42

M elissa heard her cell phone ringing. She reached behind the chair and grabbed her phone out of her purse.

"Hello?" She was surprised at the number.

"Hey girl, what up?"

"Not much. I'm still with Tricia and the rest of the girls at Mom's house. Is everything alright with you?"

"Well I was hoping you could sneak away so that we could talk. I hate to ask, but I really need you right now."

"Are you sure you're ok? You sound like something is up." Tricia asked Melissa if everything was ok.

"Don't let anyone know that you are talking to me," he whispered.

Melissa covered her phone with her hand and shook her head.

"I'm going to have to leave though. Phil is such a baby when I'm not there."

She spoke directly into the phone. "I'm leaving now. I'll call you when I get in the car." She hung up the phone. Tricia pulled Melissa to the side.

"Is Phil acting up again? You want me to call Tarik?"

Melissa smiled. "No Trish, he's cool. I'm just going to leave now and get home to help him with some things. I'll call you in the morning."

"Ok girl. Be careful." They gently hugged and Melissa left.

She started the car and put her earpiece in her ear. She hit his number and he picked up on the first ring.

"It's about time."

"Where are you?" Melissa asked in a worried tone.

"I'm near your house at the diner. Can you meet me here?"

"I'm on my way."

"Are you hungry? Do you want me to order for you?"

"Yes. Get me the usual."

Melissa parked her car right next to his jeep. She walked into the diner and found him sitting in a booth smoking a cigarette.

"Well when did you start smoking?"

"My cousin Will, just tried to throw me a bachelor party."

"What do you mean tried?" Their food arrived just as he began to speak.

"When we left the church, he suggested that we go have a drink so that I could relax. We got to this bar and all of my boys jumped up and yelled surprise. It was right on time too cause I needed get my mind off of me and Tricia's problem." Melissa ate her cheese fries while she listened. "It was going well until the strippers came out."

"Ok you must be the first man in history to not be excited about the strippers. I thought that was the best part for you men." Tarik looked up at Melissa.

"Girl, now you sound like Will. He had the nerve to get upset because I wasn't all over the strippers and shit. He asked me why I wasn't enjoying their services. I almost reached over and hooked the shit outta him. I guess I've outgrown them. Anyway, I just wanted to get away so I called you."

"You know that I'll always be here for you." Tarik called the waiter and ordered two beers.

"Don't you think that you've had enough beers at the bar?" Melissa asked.

"I guess you forgot that I'm grown, huh? Anyway, one is for you. I thought we could continue to have my bachelors party right here."

"Well, I guess it won't kill me to have one beer." They stayed at the diner until about 1:35 a.m. "Tarik, I think you should leave your car here and take a cab home. You're not in any condition to drive." They both exited the booth and went outside. They walked over to his truck and sat inside. Melissa looked at her watch. Phil would be expecting her in about thirty more minutes. "Tarik you want me to call Tricia to pick you up?"

"Nah, she's probably asleep by now. I'll just sit here a few more minutes and then drive on home."

"Now I know that you're drunk if you think that I'm going to let you drive yourself home." Tarik stared at Melissa for what seemed like forever.

"Melissa you are so beautiful."

Melissa looked over at Tarik and smirked. "I remember when you never thought of me as beautiful."

"Girl please! I've always thought of you that way. I just knew that if I told you it would make you a little uncomfortable."

"Why would I be uncomfortable? You know how much I love to hear compliments. And coming from you, that would have had me floating on cloud nine." Tarik reached over and grabbed her hand. They stared at each other for a minute. "Tarik, we have been friends for so long. I am really glad that you found someone to settle down with. I just hope we can always be as close as we are right now."

"Melissa, that will never change. I almost lost your friendship once this lifetime and I don't plan on letting that happen again. We are friends 'til the end." Tarik leaned over and pecked Melissa on the mouth. She accepted the peck. Melissa began to feel a tingle between her legs. Almost simultaneously, they grabbed each other's head and engaged in a passionate kiss. He began feeling on her breasts. Melissa let her hands wander and found herself feeling the print between his legs. She felt how large the print was and pulled away. "Tarik, we shouldn't." Tarik put two fingers to her lips and started kissing her neck. Melissa knew where this was headed but her body was saying that it was ok. *'Now if this isn't a sinful desire coming true, I don't know what is!'* Tricia thought. Tarik climbed over to Melissa's side of the truck. He pushed the seat as far back as possible. He positioned himself so that he was between Melissa's legs. Tarik undid her shirt and lifted her bra. He began sucking her breasts ever so gently. Melissa moaned in ecstasy. She pulled Tarik up to her and began kissing him hard. Tarik began to unzip his pants. He slid Melissa's skirt above her legs. Melissa knew what was happening was wrong but she wanted Tarik right then and there. Tarik entered Melissa and she gasped. He pumped in and out of her for another three minutes then he collapsed on top of her. Melissa managed to have an orgasm in the short time they engaged in sex. She kissed Tarik on his neck and rubbed his back.

"Back in high school I imagined us together but I never dreamed it would ever happen," he said between breaths. Melissa gently pushed him off of her. She was embarrassed. She silently prayed that he didn't notice the bruises on her legs. She was glad that she removed the bandage from her waist so it couldn't be seen through her clothes.

"My goodness Tarik! I can't believe we just went there."

Tarik was breathing hard. "Melissa, I didn't mean for it to happen. I just got caught up in the moment. I'm so sorry." Melissa looked out of the window. She didn't want Tarik to see the tears forming in her eyes.

"Tarik I think I better leave. Phil will be expecting me home shortly." She buttoned her shirt and pulled it down to her waist. She moved quickly to hide the bruise on her rib. Melissa reached for the door. Tarik grabbed her arm.

"Lissa wait. We need to discuss this. You can't just walk away like nothing happened."

"Tarik I can't talk about anything right now. Call me in a couple of days so we could figure this out." She opened the door and left. Tarik watched her get into her car and lean her head against the steering wheel. Melissa composed herself and drove home. Tarik started his truck and followed her to make sure she arrived home safely.

Chapter 43

M elissa walked into her house and went up to the bedroom. Phil was sitting on the floor looking over some
papers. He looked up and noticed her.

"Hey honey. Did you have a good time?" Melissa shook
her head yes as she covered her mouth to yarn.

"Yeah I had a nice time but the wine I drank is starting to
take affect. She felt dirty. She needed to take a bath. "I thought
you'd be asleep by now." She kicked off her shoes and went to
the bathroom and turned on the water.

"I was just catching up on some of the work I missed while
I was away. I'll be done in a bit."

"Ok. By the time you finish I'll be done in the bathroom."
She grabbed a pair of pajamas and went into the bathroom
and closed the door. Phil yelled through the door.

"Maybe I can join you if I'm done before you." Melissa
wiped the tears from her eyes.

"Sounds good." She sat in the hot water and cried silently
for the next ten minutes. She knew she couldn't stay in the
tub long. She did not want Phil to join her. She also knew that
he'd want to have sex tonight. There was nothing she could do
to prevent it so she had to make sure her body would be nice
and tight so he wouldn't suspect anything.

When Tarik walked through the door he noticed the time

on the cable box which read 3:35 am. He sat down on the couch and put his head in his hands and wondered how the hell he let it happen. He stood and went into the bedroom to find Tricia sound asleep. He didn't want to wake her so he went back out to the living room. The last time he checked, Tricia was still upset with him. He just wanted to put tonight behind him and marry Tricia. He contemplated if he should call Melissa, then decided he should give her a couple of days. He knew this would be the hardest two weeks of his life. He'd deal with his issues tomorrow. He went into the bathroom and took a shower.

Simone was lying across the bed reading a book when Kareem came home. He did not want to tell her that he was at a bachelor party for Tarik. She would flip knowing that she wouldn't be invited to Tricia's bridal shower. He walked into the bedroom.

"What's up Boo?"

She half-ass looked over her shoulder and mumbled, "Hey." Kareem noticed that she wasn't in bitch mode and a sigh of relief came over him.

"What you been up to all day?" he asked as he took off his boots. Simone rolled her eyes.

"I was chillin with this new friend I met at the gym." Kareem stopped and looked up.

"Word? Now dat's what's up. You need to be hanging with other people and not stressin' bout Tricia all da time." He left the room and Simone heard the shower turn on. Simone put the book down and turned off the lights. The last thing she wanted was to deal with Kareem. She lay on her back and thought *'it's funny how you can let go of someone that you love more than yourself when you're ready to.'*

Simone was tired of Kareem and she couldn't wait until Tricia's wedding so that she could tell him to get the fuck out of her life.

Chapter 44

One week before the wedding...

S helly called Simone and invited her to her apartment for
dinner. She really liked Simone and wanted to tell her the
truth about Kareem. She walked through the apartment and
made sure everything was in place. Simone rang the doorbell
and waited for Shelly to answer.

"Come on in." Shelly said as she stepped away from the
door.

"Hey girl, what's up?" Simone said as she stepped inside.

"Have a seat." Shelly offered. She was nervous as hell. She
didn't know how Simone would react but she knew she was
going to tell her everything. Shelly sat down on the sofa opposite Simone. She looked around and placed a pillow in her
lap.

"Shelly, what's up? You're acting like something's on your
mind."

"You wanna beer?" Shelly asked as she went into the
kitchen.

"Yeah, why not." Shelly returned and gave Simone a bottle of beer. "You gonna tell me or what?" Shelly sat back down.

"Simone I have to tell you something. I don't know how
you're gonna take it but I have to get this off of my chest."

Simone sat the beer on a coaster on the coffee table.

"Just tell me girl."

"Ok. When I first met you it was not by accident."

"Shelly what are you talking about? We met at the gym."

Shelly positioned herself Indian-style on the sofa.

"I don't even know where to begin."

"The beginning usually is a good place to start."

"Well there was someone I was dating right before I met you. We had just broken it off and I wanted to get revenge on him."

"Revenge for what?" Simone inquired.

"He had a girlfriend the whole time I was seeing him. I fell in love with him so he broke it off."

"Girl you are not making any sense. Talk!"

"I think I can show you better than I can tell you." Shelly reached under the end table and pulled out some pictures. She handed them to Simone and held her head down. Simone flipped through the pictures of Shelly and Kareem at different places.

"What the fuck!" Shelly stood and backed away. Are you fuckin' crazy?" Simone screamed. She looked at Shelly with tears in her eyes. Shelly walked over to Simone and sat down beside her. She reached for Simone's hand and squeezed it gently.

"Simone, just hear me out please? I know you're pissed off but I need to tell you the whole story." Simone jerked away from Shelly and stared at her for what seemed liked hours.

"When? Why?" Simone inquired.

Shelly sat back on the couch and explained her relationship with Kareem. She didn't leave out one detail. Simone sat in disbelief. Shelly didn't know what Simone was thinking. Simone sat very still for the next few minutes. She didn't want to believe what Shelly had just told her. She leaned over and hugged Simone.

"I'm so sorry Simone. We have gotten so close over the past few weeks and I didn't want you to find out any other way. And since you've been talking about dumping Kareem anyway, I thought I was helping you see that he ain't shit." Simone just shook her head like she was trying to wake up from a dream. She knew Kareem cheated on her with other women but she never thought she'd actually be face to face with one of the women let alone become friends with her. Simone turned to look at Shelly and suddenly felt a strange feeling come over her. It was the same feeling she had the night she was intimate with Tricia.

Simone hugged Shelly for a long time. She began to caress Shelly's breast. When Shelly didn't reject, Simone rubbed in between her legs. Shelly was actually enjoying Simone's hands. Shelly was nervous but she didn't want Simone to stop. She pulled Simone closer and kissed her full on the mouth. Simone's breathing began to increase. She lifted Shelly's tank top and sucked on her nipples. Shelly moaned and positioned herself so that Simone was on top of her. Shelly grabbed Simone's hair and ran her fingers through it. This made Simone wetter. She lowered her head and undid Shelly's shorts. Shelly pulled Simone's shirt over her head and fondled her breasts. Simone placed two fingers inside of Shelly and watched her moan in ecstasy. "Ooohh, Simone. I want you to make me cum!" Simone slid her fingers in and out of Shelly a few more times and then put her tongue right on Shelly's clitoris. Shelly arched her body so Simone could get a better taste. Shelly was enjoying the pleasure. She pushed Simone's head deeper inside her pussy. Simone wanted Shelly to taste her so she stood and removed what was left of her clothing. She pulled Shelly up face to face with her and slid her tongue inside of her mouth. Simone took Shelly's spot on the sofa and opened her legs. Shelly got down on her knees and licked the inside of Simone's thighs. Simone moaned and grabbed the back of Shelly's head.

Shelly carefully opened Simone's pussy and tongue fucked her. Simone was on cloud nine. She moaned and moved to the same pace as Shelly.

"Oh shit Shelly I'm cummin. Ooh, ooh, ooh, aahhhh. Shelly jumped on top of Simone and sat on her chest. She eased herself towards Simone's face so that Simone can tongue-fuck her. Simone raised her head and used her tongue the same way Kareem had done her over the years. Shelly moved faster after a few minutes. She reached her climax. Shelly breathed hard for a few moments then slid down to the floor. Simone sat up and looked at Shelly.

"You ok?"

Shelly smiled at Simone. "I'm good. Are you ok?"

Simone shook her head yes. "Was this your first time?"

"Yeah," Shelly answered. They both sat in an awkward silence for about twenty minutes. Simone was the first to speak.

"Shelly, I just thought of a way to get back at Kareem's ass."

Shelly looked up. "What you got in mind?" Shelly walked to her linen closet and grabbed two towels. She put one around her body then gave the other to Simone. She sat next to Simone on the sofa. Simone asked her if she wanted to accompany her to Tricia's wedding. Shelly said yes and Simone began to explain most of the plan.

Chapter 45

M elissa could not stop feeling guilty for what happened between her and Tarik. She and Tricia played phone tag all week. Her excuse for not seeing Tricia was that she and Phil were trying to repair their marriage. Melissa had spoken to Tricia last night and told her of the plans she made for the dinner party tomorrow. Melissa went downstairs to the kitchen and made Phil's breakfast. He was in the shower. She sat down at the table and wondered how she and Tarik could still be friends. He had been trying to call her all week. Melissa did not take any calls from him. She didn't know what to say to him. She placed the food in the plates and left them on the counter top.

Phil walked into the kitchen with a towel wrapped around his waist.

"Phil, why aren't you dressed? You're going to be late for work." Phil walked up to Melissa and kissed her on the mouth.

"It's Saturday. It doesn't matter what time I get there." He touched between her legs. "I wanted some of this last night but you fell asleep. I'll be damned if I go to work with a hard on all day." Melissa backed away from Phil with a smile on her face.

"Phil, what are you doing?"

Phil grabbed Melissa and laid her down on the kitchen table. Melissa felt like a slut for having sex with her husband.

She tried to enjoy the sex so Phil wouldn't ask any questions. All she could do was hope that he finished quickly and leave for work. Phil climbed on top of Melissa and sucked her breast. Her body responded instantly. She pulled him inside of her and fucked her husband right there on the table. About half an hour later, Phil was in their bathroom getting dressed. Melissa walked in.

"I guess breakfast is out, huh?"

Phil slipped on his shoes. "I just had my breakfast and I'm full. Baby I have to go." He kissed her on the mouth and walked downstairs. Melissa followed.

"Phil, what time should I expect you home tonight?"

"I'll be here by seven. I have so much to catch up on."

"Ok sweetie. Don't forget that I'm hosting the dinner party tomorrow for Tricia's bridal party and men are not allowed." She smiled at her husband.

"Ok, but tonight when I get home we finish what we started." Phil closed the door and smiled. He and Melissa were going to be fine. He would do everything in his power to see to that.

Tarik was determined to see Melissa today. They really needed to discuss what happened. If she insisted on not taking his calls then he had no choice but to make a pop visit to her house. He sat in his car and watched Phil drive off in the opposite direction. Tarik started his car and pulled into their driveway. He did not want to have a run-in with Phil. He got out and rang the doorbell. Melissa wiped her hand on a kitchen towel and went to the door.

"Phil, what did you forget?" When she opened the door she saw Tarik standing outside. "Tarik, why are you here?" He brushed past Melissa and went into the foyer.

"Because we need to talk. Why have you been avoiding me?" Melissa closed the door and tightened her robe. Tarik took a seat in one of the chairs. "Look Melissa, I feel just as bad as you for what happened. But avoiding me is not going to solve anything." Melissa sat in the chair across from Tarik.

"Tarik, I feel really bad about what we did. I can't even face Tricia. I can't believe we did this to her."

"That's why I'm here. I love Tricia with all of my heart. She doesn't have to know what happened between us. Could we just keep this to ourselves?"

"What? Did you forget that I have a husband, too? We are in the process of repairing our marriage and I do not need this to get out." Tarik put up a finger.

"What do you mean repairing your marriage?" Melissa let it slip that she and Phil were having problems. "Did he put his hands on you again?" Tarik stood and paced back and forth.

"Tarik, calm down! No, he didn't put his hands on me. We were just not seeing things eye to eye for a while. But we're better now. Anyway this is not about Phil and me. It's about you and me." Tarik sat down.

"I know. What are we going to do?"

"Well first, we're not gonna ever have sex again. I am so embarrassed. I can't believe I crossed the friendship line."

"Don't blame yourself, Lissa. We crossed the line together and I don't even know how we got there. I feel real fucked up!"

"Tarik, I have never made love in the back seat of a car. Not only do I feel cheap but I also feel like a backstabber. Tricia and I are friends."

"I know Melissa. Tricia is about to be my wife. I've been with her for seven years and I've never cheated on her."

"Tarik, how can you and I still remain friends? You know as well as I do that once sex is involved, everything changes."

"Lissa, it doesn't have to change anything as long as we both agree that it was meaningless and no feelings were involved."

"Tarik, I love you and I always will. There were no feelings involved on my part. I feel like I just committed incest with my brother."

"Then we can just put this behind us?"

"How do I look Tricia in the face from now on? Did you forget that I'm hosting the bridal party dinner tomorrow?"

"Melissa, I know I'm asking a lot but you have to act like everything is normal. We have to go back to the way we were."

"How can we call on each other again knowing what happened the last time one of us needed the other?"

"I'm not saying it's going to be easy. I look at you and feel uncomfortable too but as long as I know that it meant nothing for you, I can deal with it. I'm asking that you try to do the same thing."

"Relax Tarik, it didn't mean anything to me. You don't have to keep saying that. It never should have happened. And I'm sorry," Melissa stated.

"Stop apologizing. We made a mistake and we'll deal with it. That's what friends do. We work through issues together. Now come over here and give me a hug girl." Melissa stood and walked towards Tarik. The hug was a little uncomfortable at first. Melissa thought she would feel something other than friendship. After a few seconds she realized that she did not feel a thing but friendship. "So it's agreed that we leave this in the past?" Melissa shook her head yes.

"What would I do without you Tarik?"

"You'll never have to find out." Tarik sat back down in the chair.

"So how is everything going with you and Phil?"

"Do we have to have this conversation now?"

"Yes. Right now, so don't try to get out of it."

Melissa walked towards the steps. "Well let me go and throw some clothes on. Be right back. Melissa returned in a wrap around skirt and matching top. She sat on the sofa next to Tarik.

"Now what's on your mind?"

"You still haven't answered my question. What's to repair in your marriage? Melissa you have been so secretive and we've barely had time to talk lately. You better tell me the truth!"

Melissa looked at Tarik and smiled. "You'll never change, will you? Always trying to protect me. My marriage is fine. Phil and I separated a few weeks ago but we're back on the right track. I needed some time alone. I had to find myself. You have been telling me all these years that I no longer have an identity and I realized you were right. I needed to be my own woman again. Phil understood and gave me some space." Melissa smiled at Tarik and looked away nervously.

"Ok Melissa, if you're not going to be honest about what's going on then we can end the conversation. I'll just have to find out what's going on another way." Melissa glanced up at Tarik and frowned. "Are you calling me a liar?"

"Yes. I know you're lying, I just can't prove it right now." He stood. "I have to get to the office and check on a few things. I'll call you later. Remember what we promised."

"I will. I have to go shopping for some last minute things. I'll see you later."

"Yep." Melissa said as she closed the door behind him. She leaned against the door and hoped that she'd be able to be cool around Tricia tomorrow. She headed upstairs to the shower.

Chapter 46

K areem walked through the apartment and wondered where Simone could be. He hadn't seen much of her this past week. Tomorrow they were going to the wedding against his better judgment. He really thought Simone should stay away but there was no way he could talk her out of it. Simone came through the door and pecked him on the lips.

"What's up? Do you have everything you need for tomorrow or do we need to go to the mall?"

"Damn girl, slow down. Where you been? I barely saw you all week." She poured herself a glass of lemonade and sat at the kitchen table.

"I've been busy with work and making sure I have everything for the wedding. Do you need anything?" Kareem sat at the table with her.

"Nah, I'm straight. I'll just go and pick up some black socks later." Simone drank the last of her lemonade and headed to the bedroom. Kareem followed. He walked up behind Simone and grabbed her waste.

"Kareem, get off of me. What are you doing?"

Kareem frowned. "I was tryna get some play. You been holding out on me all week. What's up?" Simone turned her back to him and turned her nose up. The thought of having sex with him made her nauseous; especially since she knew he used to fuck Shelly. She hasn't been intimate with Kareem in weeks. She didn't want to make him suspicious so she faced him with a wicked smile. "I just came from the gym so let me take a shower first." He returned her wicked smile. "Aiight. You handle yo business in there and I'll handle some business out here. Hurry up, baby."

Simone went into the bathroom and smiled. She stood under the water and her mind drifted to last night. She and Shelly had had sex again and again. She knew this would be her last time fucking Kareem so she'd send him out with a smile. He had no idea this would be the last night he'd spend in their apartment.

• • •

Tricia pulled into her mother's driveway. Mrs. Hobbs met her at the door. She took the bags from Tricia and put them in the house.

"Tricia are you still going to get Melissa so she could stay over, too?" Tricia's mind was in a daze.

"Tricia you hear me talking to you girl?" Tricia jerked her head around.

"I'm sorry momma. What did you say?"

"Is Melissa still coming?"

"No. She's going to come over early in the morning. She had to run some errands today, then she and Phil have plans tonight."

"Ok. Well we have a nail appointment in an hour." Mrs. Hobbs hopped in Tricia's car and clicked her seatbelt.

"Trish, let's go to the mall first. I need to get a pair of pantyhose. I don't want those cheap ones they sell in the corner store." Tricia started the car and drove off.

They returned to Mrs. Hobbs house at five forty p.m. Tricia sat on the sofa exhausted. Mrs. Hobbs went to the kitchen and bought back a bottle of wine and two glasses. She filled one glass and handed it to Tricia.

"I know you can use a drink, baby." Tricia looked at her

mother with tears in her eyes.

"Thanks Mommy." Mrs. Hobbs sat in the recliner.

"What's wrong, Trish?"

Tricia wiped her eyes. "Momma, I'm so happy. But I'm nervous as hell. I want to marry Tarik more than anything in the world but what if something goes wrong?" Mrs. Hobbs sipped from her glass. She smiled at Tricia.

"Honey, it's ok to be nervous. Hell, if you weren't nervous, I'd think something was wrong with you. I am so proud of you. You have become a wonderful beautiful woman. You found yourself a man who loves you unconditionally. Your father was very proud of you too."

"Momma, stop getting all emotional on me."

"Tricia, you are my only baby and you have grown up to be your own woman. Just remember one thing about marriage. It's give and take. You'll have to compromise for the rest of your life. This means you can't come running over here leaving your husband every time you two don't agree." Tricia laughed. "I'm not saying that you're no longer welcome, but your place is with your husband. I'm sure Tarik knows by now that you are as stubborn as ever but he loves you anyway. I know you'll be a good wife and friend. But if you don't listen to anything I say, believe me when I say, never lose yourself, chile."

Tricia wiped her face and went to give her mother a hug and kiss. "I love you Ma. And thanks for the speech."

"I figure you'd rather hear it now than at the wedding." They both laughed and drank the rest of the wine.

The doorbell rang and Tricia went to the window. She opened the door.

"Tarik, what are you doing here? You are not supposed to see me before tomorrow."

Tarik walked into the house. "Hi Moms."

"Hello darling. What are you doing here?" she asked with raised eyes. Tricia closed the door.

"I need to talk to Trish before we get married. There's something I'd like to tell her." Tricia blushed and sat on the sofa. Mrs. Hobbs went upstairs.

"Tricia." Tarik said as he sat down next to her and held both her hands. "I just want to let you know that I love you very much. We have overcome some tough obstacles this year. I'm glad that I have you to share my life with. I can't wait to make you my wife tomorrow. See you at the church. I love you, Boo." Tricia was wiping her eyes as Tarik stood to leave.

"I love you too, Tarik. And I can't wait to become your wife tomorrow. I hope you had fun at your bachelor party last week. Now get out of here before we start something we can't finish. She smiled at the look on Tarik's face. Tarik blew her a kiss and walked out of the house. *'How did she know about the party?'*

Tricia was too nervous to sleep. She went over her vows a few more times.

Melissa paced back and forth in her bedroom. She pulled through the dinner party last weekend but how was she going to stand beside Tricia tomorrow at the wedding. She still felt uncomfortable being near her. She couldn't understand why because she didn't have a problem being around Tarik. She just chalked it up as being a woman thing. She replayed her conversation with Tarik in her head over and over. *'As long as feelings weren't involved then everything will be okay.'* She knew Tarik was right. He was her friend and she owed him at least to do her part at the wedding. There is nothing that he wouldn't do for her. Phil walked into the bedroom interrupting her thoughts.

"Hey baby. You okay?"

Melissa smiled at her husband. "Yes sweetie, I'm fine. Are you all ready for tomorrow?" Phil sat on the bed next to her.

"Yeah baby, I'm all set. But there's something I want to talk to you about." Melissa moved to the back of the bed and pushed herself up against the headboard. "What's on your mind?"

"How do you feel about taking a vacation real soon?"

"Phil, I have to go back to work next Monday. I've been off for two months already. I don't want to lose my job." Phil took off his shoes and moved towards Melissa.

"I know baby but you don't really need that job. Why don't you take a leave of absence and stay at home for a while."

Melissa wrinkled her nose. "I thought we agreed that I can work if I wanted. I like my job and it gives me something to do while you're working and going out of town all the time. Anyway, why are you suggesting this?"

"Well, I just think that you and I could use some time together. I want you and I to have a new start. Let's concentrate on getting our marriage back on the right track before you return to work." Melissa was speechless. Whenever Phil suggested something, it meant that it was his way or no way. She wanted to know if Phil was genuine or not about his change. She decided to be a little difficult to see where Phil's head was.

"Phil, I don't think that me working is going to prevent us from getting our marriage on the right track." Phil's eyes got smaller. He was trying to remain calm with Melissa but he didn't know how much longer he could let her talk to him this way. He was not used to this take-charge attitude. He was the one who said what goes and what doesn't. He bit his tongue.

"Baby, maybe you could think about it and we can discuss it further after the wedding tomorrow." Melissa pulled the comforter back and lay in the bed.

"Okay Phil. I'll think about it and we can discuss it later."

"That's all I ask, baby." He kissed Melissa on the mouth and walked towards the door.

"Aren't you coming to bed, Phil?"

"In a few. I'm going downstairs to do some work."

"Okay hon, I'll probably be asleep when you get back so good-night."

"Night Lissa." Phil went into the kitchen and opened the cupboard and got a glass. He went to his briefcase and removed a pint of Hennessey. He pushed the glass aside and put the bottle to his mouth. Phil would go up to his bedroom four hours later. Drunk.

Chapter 47

The wedding day.........

Melissa woke Phil and gave him directions to the church. She put the information on the refrigerator and grabbed her garment bag.

"Phil I'm leaving, I'll see you later. Please be on time. The ceremony will start at noon." Phil sat up. His head was spinning. He had a hangover.

"Melissa, I'll be there on time. It's only seven-thirty why are you waking me so early?"

"I needed to give you the directions and let you know that I was leaving. Tricia will be here any minute so we won't have to take two cars. I'll ride with you to the reception."

"Melissa, call me at ten forty-five to wake me please. I'm so tired." Phil pulled the covers over his head.

"Bye, sweetie."

Phil mumbled something as Melissa ran down stairs to a blowing car horn. Tricia jumped out of the car and sat on the passenger side.

"I guess I'm driving, huh?" Melissa said as she adjusted the seat and mirror. "What's up girl? Are you ready to become a wife today or what?" Tricia burst into tears. This made Melissa nervous. She thought Tricia might have known something.

"What's wrong, honey? Why are you crying?" Tricia grabbed some napkins from the glove compartment and wiped her face.

"Melissa, I'm so nervous. What if something goes wrong? Will everyone come?"

"Calm down sweetie. You have every right to be nervous. But you don't have anything to worry about. Your mother and I will be right there with you. It's natural for you to be nervous but you have to stop all this crying and stuff. We are not going to the wedding with red eyes. There's not enough makeup in the world to cover a puffy face. You are going to look beautiful and your wedding is going to be wonderful."

Tricia smiled at Melissa. "That's why I love you, Melissa. You always know just what to say." Melissa looked straight ahead and began to feel bad again.

"You okay, Lissa? Why are you looking down?"

Melissa turned to Tricia. "Uh uh. This is your day. It's about you. We can discuss me next week sometime." They laughed and talked until they reached the beauty parlor where all the women in the wedding were taking turns under the dryers.

• • •

Mrs. Hobbs put all the food in the car and headed towards the ballroom. She spent the last two days preparing food. Tricia's wedding day was going to be perfect and the food was going to be delicious. She hung her dress in the rear of the car and drove off.

Simone woke Kareem at ten thirty.

"Let's get moving Kareem. We don't want to be late. My girl is getting married in a couple of hours." Kareem looked at Simone like she was crazy.

"Simone, are you sure you wanna go through with this. Tricia made it perfectly clear that she didn't want you there."

"Kareem don't start tripping now. Get ready! 'Cause we're going! And I may even have a surprise for you later on." She smiled and went into the bathroom.

"What kind of surprise?" He yelled through the bathroom door.

Shelly walked into her closet and pulled out the dress she and Simone picked out at the mall earlier this week. She put her pantyhose and shoes next to the bed, and then went to the shower thinking about Simone. Shelly could think of nothing else since she and Simone first had sex. She didn't know this feeling but if Simone were a man, Shelly would be in love. Or is she in love.

The wedding..........

Tricia and Melissa were sitting in a room waiting for the right time to get dressed. Melissa peeked out the door a few times to see if Phil had arrived. She spotted him at eleven forty-five. She had one of the ushers escort him to the back of the church where she was.

"Hi honey. Thank you for being here on time." He gave her a hug.

"I told you not to worry that I'd be here on time. I'm going to my seat. I'll see you after the ceremony." They kissed and he left.

Melissa entered the room and looked at Tricia.

"You okay?" Tricia nodded yes. "Good. It's time to get you married."

Tricia wiped the tears from her eyes and stood in the mirror. "Help me with the dress over my head, please?"

"Of course, I'm going to help you. That's why I'm here."

Mrs. Hobbs walked in the room. "Tricia, it's time to walk down the aisle. The music began and Melissa walked out and down the aisle. "You look beautiful, baby. Let's go get you married."

The traditional "Here Comes The Bride" rang loud through the speakers. Tricia put her arm through her mothers' and was escorted down the aisle. The bridesmaids all smiled when they saw the tears in Tricia's eyes. Everyone stood and was awed as she made her way to Tarik, who was standing next to Will with his hands locked in front of him. Mrs. Hobbs reached Tarik and gave her baby to him. Tricia looked over at Melissa and smiled. Melissa winked her eye and smiled back. Melissa took a quick glance through the crowd and noticed the smile on Phil's face. She blew a kiss at her husband and turned her attention back to the wedding.

Sabrina stepped out of the bridesmaids line and walked directly in front of Tricia and Tarik.

"This song is from the bottom of my heart. I love you guys." She began to sing Monica's 'For You I Will'. Sabrina's voice had everyone in the church in tears. She sang the song acapella. She didn't miss one note and the song was beautiful. When she was done, she put the mic back in its place and hugged Tricia and Tarik. "Now get married." She whispered as she took her spot with the bridesmaids.

Simone and Kareem walked in the church as Sabrina received a standing ovation. They took a seat in the back of the church. The minister gave Tricia the sign to recite her vows to Tarik. She recited her handwritten vows, while Tarik held her hand. Melissa wiped the tears from Tricia's eyes as she read from the paper. It was now Tarik's turn to recite his vows. Will passed him the paper and he began to talk to Tricia. She cried even harder as Tarik proclaimed his love for her. Melissa tried her best to keep Tricia's face dry to avoid ruining her make up.

Simone kept looking back towards the exit wondering where the hell Shelly could be.

"I'm going to the bathroom, Kareem. Be right back."

"Simone how are you going to get up in the middle of the ceremony?" She pulled from his grip.

"I have to use the restroom," she said through gritted teeth. She disappeared behind the doors.

The minister looked out into the church of people and spoke loudly. "If there is anyone here who thinks this man and woman should not be married, will you speak now or forever hold your peace." Simone walked into the church with Shelly tailing behind her. Kareem's mouth dropped open. Shelly took a seat in the last row and winked at Kareem. Simone walked down the aisle towards Tricia and Tarik. There were some whispers and finger pointing.

"Simone why are you here? I asked you to stay away." It was so quiet that everyone heard Tricia's whisper. "How else was I able to get your attention? You wouldn't even talk to me. We are friends until the end." Mrs. Hobbs went up to Simone and grabbed her hand. She whispered in Simone's ear. "What the hell is wrong with you girl? You are ruining her wedding. Now I know you're hurting chile, but if you really care about Tricia you would just leave now and we'll get together to discuss this at another time." Simone looked at Mrs. Hobbs with tears in her eyes. Kareem walked down the aisle and pulled Simone from behind.

"Simone what the hell are you doing?" The minister cleared his throat and looked at Kareem. "Simone, you are embarrassing yourself. Let's go!" He managed to push Simone out of the church. Tricia stood there crying like a baby. Melissa was right by her side telling her that everything was going to be okay. Mrs. Hobbs went over to Tarik and Tricia and took their hands. "Everything is fine. Let's go get y'all married." Tarik embraced Tricia and led her towards the minister. "Reverend, please continue. This was just a misunderstanding. Everything's all right now." Mrs. Hobbs then faced the people in the church. "Will everyone please sit so that we can go on with the ceremony?" Everyone sat in their seats and took their places.

The reverend continued to marry Tarik and Tricia. The bridesmaids were looking back to see if Simone would return. Melissa stood right by Tricia's side and continued to wipe her face.

"I now pronounce you husband and wife. You may kiss your bride." Tarik lifted Tricia's vail and kissed her passionately on the mouth. Tricia turned around and hugged Melissa and thanked her for being by her side.

Just as the newlyweds were about to jump over the broom, there was commotion in the aisle. Kareem ran down the aisle to catch Simone. He yelled for her to stop but she continued to run to the front of the church. He finally caught up to her and they tussled. He tried to remove the gun from her hand but her grip was too strong. None of the guests saw that she had a gun. Kareem grabbed her hand and got a grip on the gun. Two shots were fired before the gun landed on the floor. People began to duck under pews and scream for help. Tricia was pulled to the floor. Tarik ran through the crowd towards Simone. Tricia called his name and tried to get up from the floor but there was something stopping her. Melissa's bloody body was laid across her legs.

"Oh my goodness. She's been shot!"

Mrs. Hobbs ran to Tricia.

"Trish? My baby's been shot!" She knelt down on the floor next to Tricia and cried.

"No Mama, Melissa was shot!

Phil pushed his way through the crowd as he heard that Melissa was shot. He reached Melissa and saw the blood seeping through her stomach. "Tricia, please don't move. We can't move her until the paramedics arrive. Phil flipped open his phone and dialed 911.

Tarik left the crowd that surrounded Simone when the shots were fired. He saw the crowd and pushed his way through.

"Trish? Trish? Where are you?" Phil stopped Tarik and told him that Tricia was fine.

"Let me go, Phil. I need to get to my wife." Phil stood in front of Tarik to block his view.

"Tarik, she's fine. Melissa's been shot and I need your help. You have to stay calm!"

Phil took off his jacket and placed it against Melissa's stomach. Phil looked up, "Tarik, I need you to hold this here against her stomach." Tarik couldn't move. He couldn't believe that Melissa was lying there bleeding.

"I'll do it." Tricia grabbed the jacket and held it to Melissa. Tears were streaming from her eyes but she was as calm as she could be. She whispered in Melissa's ear, "Lissa, don't you die on us. You can do this. You can pull through this. Just hold on until we get you to the hospital. You're going to be fine. It's not your time, Lissa."

Phil knelt down next to Tricia and gently placed his hands under Melissa's neck. He very tenderly held her body and told Tricia to slide back so that Melissa could be propped up. Tricia did as Phil instructed. She never let go of Melissa's hand.

"Where is the damn ambulance?" Phil yelled. "Melissa baby, please don't die. I need you! I can't make it without you, baby." The paramedics pushed through the crowd and Phil gave them a report on Melissa. They started an IV and put her on the stretcher. Phil followed as he held Melissa's hand. Tricia went to Tarik and grabbed his hand. They hopped in the limo and followed the ambulance to the hospital. Mrs. Hobbs stayed with the guests to try and calm them down. All of the guests were instructed by the police that they needed to stay for questioning.

Epilogue

P hil was in the hospital room with his wife. Tarik paced the floor of the waiting room. Tricia sat in a chair wearing her bloody wedding gown. She'd been crying for the past five hours. Tarik went to the nurses' station for the fourth time and asked how Melissaa was doing. The nurse told him that she wasn't able to give him any information at this time.

"Well get someone out here who can tell me what the hell is going on!" The nurse looked frightened and pushed the button for security. Tricia went to Tarik and hugged him tightly.

"Baby, it's not her fault. She's only doing her job. Stop yelling at her." She escorted him to the chair and laid his head on her shoulder. Tarik cried like a baby. The security officer arrived and the nurse explained the situation. He asked Tarik and Tricia to leave.

Tarik stood. "We're not going anywhere! My sister has been shot and no one will tell us what's going on. I'd like to see you put me outta here tonight." Tricia stood in front of Tarik and apologized for his behavior. Just as the officer was about to speak, Dr. Michael Carter and Phil walked up to them.

"Officer, it's okay. We'll take it from here." Dr. Carter led them to a small office. "Guys, Melissa has lost a lot of blood but she pulled through the surgery and has just regained consciousness. She and the baby are going to be just fine." Tarik, Tricia, and Phil looked at each other and in unison yelled, "Baby!"

Tricia looked at Phil. "She never mentioned that she was

pregnant."

Dr. Carter looked at them all. "She probably didn't know yet. You all can go back and see her in a few hours." Phil looked at the floor and tried to hold back the tears.

Tarik walked towards Phil. "Congratulations, man. Lissa told me that y'all were tryna have a baby."

Phil accepted Tarik's handshake and half smiled. "Thanks, man."

Tricia thanked Dr. Carter and went to Phil. "Melissa is going to be surprised to find out that she's pregnant."

"Not as surprised as I am." Phil said solemnly and walked out of the room.

EXCERPT FROM THE SEQUEL:

With Friends Like That

Chapter 1

S imone and Kareem sat side by side on one of the pews. Simone continually cried on his shoulders. She never meant for anyone to get hurt. When an officer stood in front of them for questioning, he informed them that the entire guest list agreed that Simone caused a scene. He told them that they could answer questions now or they can wait to have an attorney present.

Mrs. Hobbs went to Simone and told her not to say anything without a lawyer.

"But moms, we don't have anything to hide," Kareem said.

"Moms, I didn't mean for any of this to happen."

"I know baby but that's not the case. That chile was shot and all fingers are pointing at you. I don't know what happened back there but this does not look good for you. Kareem, y'all keep your mouths shut!" The officer asked Mrs. Hobbs not to discuss any more details with Simone and Kareem. He moved them to the back of the church where there were officers guarding the door. Simone held Kareem's hand and squeezed as tight as she could. Kareem looked around the church to see if anyone was in earshot before he spoke.

"Simone, we're gonna be ok. We just won't say anything until we get a lawyer." She continued to cry.

"Kareem, I'm scared. I don't wanna go to jail. I feel so bad for Melissa. I...I...didn't mean for this to happen," she said between sniffles.

"I know baby." He looked around again. He shook her and made her face him. "Simone, we can't be sure who shot Melissa. We both had our hands on the gun and it just went off. No one can prove that either of us shot her. But, if it comes down to that, I'll take the blame." She looked up at Kareem.

"What? Kareem I don't want you to go to jail either. We're not going to lie."

"Simone, please trust me on this. We are going to be fine. It was an accident. Even if I take the fall for this, there's not too much they can do to me." She shook her head no. She reached into her purse and grabbed some tissues. She used it to wipe her face dry. She squeezed Kareem's hands a little tighter.

"Kareem I can't let you take the fall for something that I did. I'm going to have to face my responsibilities for a change."

"What you mean by that?"

"I mean that it's time for me to take some blame in this whole fiasco. I went too far."

"Simone, where did you get that gun anyway?"

"I bought it from a shop a few weeks ago."

"Why would you buy a gun if you wasn't planning to use it?" She looked at him and wiped more tears from her face.

"Hey," Shelly said as she touched Simone's shoulder.

"Hi Shelly."

"Are you ok?"

Simone shook her head yes.

"The officer said that I could talk to you for five minutes." Kareem looked at Shelly with rage in his eyes. He was trying to figure out how they knew each other. Simone turned her body slightly away from Kareem and faced Shelly.

"I'm sorry Shelly. Things got a little out of control. I would never have invited you if I would have known all of this was gonna happen.

"I know sweetie."

"Invite her? What the hell are you talking about Simone? How do y'all know each other?" he asked as he stood up in front of Simone.

"I could ask you the same thing, couldn't I?" She said in a sarcastic tone.

Shelly looked at Kareem and revealed a wicked smile.

Chapter 2

M elissa opened her eyes and wondered where she was. She lifted her head and looked around the room suspiciously. A sharp pain shot through her stomach and caused her to yell out. Within seconds, a nurse was by her side.

"What's wrong Mrs. Monroe?"

Melissa spoke softly as she grabbed her stomach.

"I'm in pain. My stomach is killing me."

"Well, that's going to happen for a while after what you've been through."

"What does that mean? Mrs....? I'm sorry, I didn't get your name."

"Oh, I'm nurse Gordon. I'll get the doctor in here to explain things to you." Nurse Gordon proceeded to put pain medication through Melissa's IV then left the room. Melissa tried to sit up but quickly realized that she didn't have the strength. She fumbled around until she found the bed button. She raised her head. She touched her stomach and tried to rub the pain away. Just as she closed her eyes, Dr. Michael Carter entered the room.

"How's it going, Lissa?" She pulled the sheets above her breasts and smiled in embarrassment.

"You tell me. I'm in so much pain." Dr. Carter pulled a chair up and sat next to Melissa.

"Do you remember being shot?"

"No, I was shot? When, Who did it?" She couldn't get all of the questions out fast enough.

"Lissa, do you remember anything within the past twenty four hours?" She frowned her forehead and closed her eyes.

"I remember I was standing next to Tricia, at the wedding." Images of the wedding were coming back to her. "I remember Simone caused a lot of confusion. Oh my goodness, did she shoot me?"

"Calm down Melissa!" Dr. Carter said as he forced her to lie down. Melissa lay back on the bed. She began to replay the events in her head. She looked at Michael.

"What happened to Tricia and Tarik?"

"I need you to relax. Everyone is out front waiting to see you." She smiled then asked if they could come in.

"I have to discuss some things with you before I let them back here."

"Ok. I'm listening. How much damage was done?" She asked in pain.

He sat back in the chair and wrote something in her chart.

"Obviously, you were shot in the stomach. You've lost a lot of blood, but you will be ok." She sighed in relief. She looked at him with tears in her eyes. She couldn't believe that she'd been shot.

"There's more, Melissa."

"How much worse can this get?"

He fidgeted with her chart for a moment before he spoke.

"Melissa, you're pregnant. You're very lucky that your body didn't abort the fetus. Normally, in this kind of situation you would have lost the baby." There was a pause before he spoke again.

"I recommend that you see an OB/GYN immediately. You are a high risk pregnancy." Dr. Carter noticed that Melissa didn't respond.

"Are you ok, Melissa?"

"Mike, this is the happiest day in my life. Phil and I have been trying to have a baby for months. We are finally going to have the family that we've been working for." Dr. Carter stared at Melissa before he spoke again.

"I told your husband already. He and your friends have known for a few hours now. I thought they knew already. I hope you don't mind me telling them before I told you."

"Please Mike, don't be silly. They're my family. I'm going to send out notices as soon as I can." She laughed so hard that she made her stomach hurt. Michael Carter half smiled.

"When am I getting out of here?"

"Well, you are going to have to stay for a few more days for observation but we'll talk on Thursday." She smiled and thanked him.

"Now let me go get your husband in here." He walked towards the door and turned to face her. "Let me be the first to congratulate you on the good news." Melissa couldn't control her excitement. She had the biggest cheese smile on her face. "I'll be back to talk with you later, but if you need me before then, just call."

"Will do." She said as she patted her stomach.

• • •

Tricia tapped carefully on the door before pushing it open. She went to Melissa and grabbed both of her hands. Melissa squeezed Tricia's hands and began to cry.

"I'm so sorry that the wedding didn't go as planned, Trish." Tricia sat on the side of the bed.

"Lissa, it wasn't your fault. You did everything right. I'm sorry for what happened to you."

Melissa wiped her eyes.

"No. Simone did this, not you. I would never blame you for what she did. How is she anyway?"

Tricia looked away with tears in her eyes. Melissa changed the subject.

"Well, at least you still get to be an auntie." She sang as she rubbed her belly.

"Mike told me how lucky I am to still have the baby."

"Yeah, that is amazing. Mr. Hammond and I are truly happy for you and Phil."

"I don't remember you guys saying I do."

Tricia raised an eyebrow.

"I told you that nothing was going to stop me from becoming Mrs. Tarik Hammond." Melissa frowned from the pain in her stomach.

"Are you okay? You need me to get a doctor?"

"No. I'll be ok. It's just that I'm trying to turn on my side." Tricia helped Melissa turn on her side.

"I wish this pain medication would hurry up and kick in. Tricia, where's Phil?" Tricia walked over to the window. She sighed and kept her back to Melissa.

"Well, when Dr. Carter came out and told us that you were pregnant, Phil walked out of the room. Tarik has had him paged twice but he hasn't responded. Tarik went to the cafeteria to see if he were there, but he wasn't."

Melissa had a confused look on her face. "I guess the news that we're having a baby shocked him." Tricia returned to Melissa's bedside. Melissa tried to conceal her disappointment. She smiled at Tricia before she spoke. "He's probably out buying cigars or something." Tricia looked away and twirled her fingers in her hair.

Tarik opened the door carrying all kinds of balloons and teddy bears. Melissa smiled when she saw him.

"You are too silly Tarik." She managed a smile. Tarik knelt down to give her a hug.

"Hey hon, how you feel?"

"I'm told I'll survive."

"Good!" You had us all scared for a minute there."

"Yeah, imagine how I felt." Everyone laughed. Tarik went over and kissed Tricia on the lips.

"Hey Boo, how are you doing?"

"I'm fine." She stood and allowed him to sit down so that she could sit on his lap. She tried to be enthusiastic when she spoke. She was trying hard to cheer up Melissa. "I was just telling Lissa how great it is that she and Phil are having a baby."

Melissa looked up with a grin on her face. "I'm so excited! I can't wait to be a mommy."

Tarik's whole attitude changed.

"Well, I'm not so sure that now is a good time for you two to start a family." Tricia stood.

"Tarik, why would you say something like that?"

Melissa glared at him. "It's ok Tricia. That's his way of being subtle. He never could bite his tongue. I'm used to his shit!"

Tarik and Tricia stared at each other.

"Melissa calm down. I'm sure Tarik didn't mean it like that."

Tarik sat on the side of the bed.

"Lissa, you know I love you and only want what's best for you. Look at the situation. You've just been shot! Where the hell is Phil? The only place he should be is right here by your side. He just found out that he's going to be a father and he's not here with you? Come on now. Stop making excuses for him!"

Tricia took Tarik by the arm and led him to the door. "Boo, go outside and cool off. Let me talk to Lissa alone for a minute." Tarik blocked the door with his arm. "I'm not going anywhere Tricia. She needs to hear what I'm gonna say!"

Melissa pulled the cord for the nurse.

"Excuse me, please." Nurse Gordon said as she entered the room. "You called, is everything ok Mrs. Monroe?"

Melissa used a tissue to wipe her eyes and sniffed a few times. "I would like to be left alone, please. I don't want to see anyone except for my husband. Would you please escort my *friends* out of my room?" She lowered her bed and closed her eyes. The nurse asked Tricia and Tarik to follow her as she left the room.

"Melissa, please let me stay and talk to you." Tricia pleaded.

"We'll talk later Trish. I just want to rest right now." Melissa said with her face turned away from Tricia. Tricia backed out of the room and glared at Tarik.

Melissa tried to stop the tears from falling. The last thing she wanted was for Tarik not to be happy for her. This pregnancy was the one thing she's wanted for three years. She wondered why he wouldn't just accept the fact that She and Phil would be together for a long time. Sleep carried her away before she could complete all of her thoughts.

Chapter 3

P hil paced the living room of he and Melissa's home for what seemed like hours. He knew he should've been at the hospital with his wife but he couldn't get past the shock of her being pregnant. He tried to understand how it happened. He was very careful when they made love. He knew it was wrong but he only told Melissa they could start a family to shut her up. Now he is facing the fact that he's going to be a father at forty—five years old. He finally sat down on the sofa and picked up the phone. He called the hospital and asked for his wife's number. The operator transferred him to her room.

"Hello?" she asked unsure of who could be calling.

"Hey honey. How are you doing?" Melissa raised the bed so that she could talk on the phone.

"Hi sweetie, where are you?" He re-positioned himself on the sofa.

"I'm at home, baby. I'll be there in a little while."

She smiled, "Why aren't you here now? It would have been nice if my husband's face were the first I saw when I opened my eyes."

Phil sighed loudly. "Melissa, I'll be there in a few. I'm leaving now! He waited for her to respond. "Ok. I'll see you when you get here." Phil hung up the phone and went into the kitchen and poured himself a double shot of Hennesy.

Melissa hung up the phone and tried to fight her tiredness. The pain medication had finally taken affect. She was asleep within minutes. She awakened twelve hours later with no sign of her husband.

Also by Ty Goode

His Baggage Her Load
ISBN # 0-9758602-1-6
$14.95

With Friends Like That...
ISBN # 0-9758602-2-4
$14.95